Friendly Advice

Aftermath

Craig Kanyemba

Friendly Advice: Aftermath

Published by Apadana Group
info@craigkanyemba.co.za
www.craigkanyemba.co.za
Reg. 2018/618735/07
Johannesburg, South Africa

Books
Shepherd and the lost sheep: A Motherless Child
Against All Odds: A Road to United States of Africa

Also available on Amazonkindle and Smashwords

ISBN 978-0-620-81354-9

eISBN 978-0-620-81354-9

First published in 2018

Layout and cover design by Apadana Group

Design Artist - Nico Meyer

Printed in South Africa by Digital Action

To my Lord, my God, a second letter to you
Thank you everyone for your further support:

My family and all my friends,
I really appreciate all of you.

About the Author

Craig Kanyemba is a writer of six books, contemporary fiction novels and non-fiction works. He is an activist born in Zimbabwe, and his work attributes and contributes to the fight against modern oppression through his story telling skills.

Contents

"Whatever I tell you in the dark, speak in the light; and what you hear in the ear, preach on the housetops. And do not fear those that kill the body but cannot kill the soul. But rather fear Him who is able to destroy both soul and body in hell. Are not two sparrows sold for a copper coin? And not one of them fall to the ground apart from your Father's will. But the very hairs of your head are all numbered. Do not fear therefore; you are of more value than many sparrows.

Chapter 01 - The Past

A vast sun-scorched plain stretching away in endless miles under a blazing sky. FEW MONTHS HAD PASSED, Jadea's thigh had healed from a wound and all he kept on thinking about was his stolen car. It is immensely gratifying that he loved material objects and to some extent, he felt like it granted him certain power over others. He hoped to aggrandize himself by dying a hero's death.

Stanley Ncube, Jadea's cousin never stopped denying accusation laid upon him when he tried and was unsuccessful to debunk Stanley Ncube's involvement in all this.

When they shot him and robbed his car, they left him badly wounded. Jadea had asked him a few times about it, but Foster did not change his statement and he persistently denied the allegations. He became rebarbative and prickly and spiteful.

> This life we have submitted to treats us like a lost and abandoned dog. Leadership methods are wickedly endogenic, when one voice speaks out loud, it is either paid to shut up or a scissor could be used to slit wide open that throat to stop vocals. So, to that a witty impromptu must not sound premeditated.

BOTH OF THEM HAD HEALED from their bullet wounds, but this did not mean they were changing their ways of life. Six months had passed after the death of the former Detective Petrus Mduduzi. These two cousins took a new turn after spending months trying to find their stolen vehicles.

Flustered Foster found a solution to end the bad blood between them. He explained to Jadea that his stolen car was long gone and sold. Jadea had a vigilant heart and couldn't accept losses. To him, this was a cycle of reprisal and retaliation. He lived night and day with the incessant voices and a will of ruthless revenge.

TEMPESTUOUS overwhelms when answers are futile. In such episodic moments, it was hard to notice the catastrophes that emerged from negative enthusiasm. Foster had no-idea about Tanya's whereabouts since they did part-ways. Foster took both cars from Tanya and left him with nothing except his underwear.

He told Jadea about Tanya's sister since Foster knew that the robbery that happened to his cousin was propagated by Tanya. He angled his way into Tanya's life. The same week Jadea started knowing about the sister, he visited her. At some point, Tanya had to face some retribution.

> Most people smile instead of being subversive as they are tossed around like a gambling coin and then speaks out behind closed doors. A bad leader steals from his own people until they run into another neighbour for safety. Some stole money and different things, but the one who steals people's lives is none other than a fallen angel himself. Revolutionaries are butchered like a sheep and for a pittance some were bought.

He asked around for her address like an analytic rigour, from place to place, he was unfortunate at first. He wanted the young man to face the repercussions of all his acts. Jadea saw a razor blade in Tanya's eyes, and yet, he failed to notice a long blade in his own eye.

Months went-by after Neil had witnessed someone being stabbed on a pavement. This changed his whole perspective about life, he dropped out of college just after failing to meet assignments dates and exam requirements, without an existing repertoire, his short-term relationship girlfriend was pregnant, and she needed him to provide paternal care. With no wisdom about being a father, he was left with no choice but to face the aftermath.

He moved back into his mother's house located in high density locations where many of his friends were still doing drugs. To them, he claimed that the drug life was all behind him. Needlessly, his craving for drugs grew deeper and deeper, while unaware he found himself in a tunnel of addiction without any hope of escaping.

He started hanging around again with those that shared the same habits and same baby problems with him. Whenever his pregnant girlfriend complained about his bad attitude towards her, he would go back to his old brothers to snort and smoke. They felt blessed and ungrateful together.

> Everything will seem so little and inconsequential after seeing armies marching to mud and death, and people will soon get tired of hearing about that. Public, either fears to encourage and join in to conquer as a whole, so it steps aside and watches in tears as babies are ripped out of wombs or the same public further mocks the courageous and despise their words arrogantly. In the end people feel impotent rage.

Neil found a job at a local restaurant, but he couldn't bear the hard work or workplace regulations. His laziness was conveyed into anger against his prosperous-looking colleagues. He was not motivated, which led him to make a number of wrong orders. His manager tried to push him in line. He couldn't see any light at the end of the tunnel, he gave up the job to sit around with his buddies during the day doing nothing.

Most of them had given up on their dreams, and they were looking for more recruits to join in on drug abuse. The desperations of money had hooked his thoughts like a pandemonium.

TAMMY'S BELLY WAS growing bigger and bigger as days and weeks were passing by. Since she told him about her pregnancy and her need to raise the baby with him, he felt this as nothing but a burden. He told her to abort the baby several times. He knew by every means that this child was his, although, the girl he was about to have a baby with knew nothing else besides clubs and celebrities. She fell pregnant at a very young age.

He knew they'd had sex a few times without protection. It was hard for him to believe the word of her mouth. Another night, she cried out loud suggesting if they would take a DNA test to prove it after the baby is born. She was perfectly sure this child belonged to him.

> Nothing profitable comes out of business deals with poor ethics. A time comes when a visitor overstays his welcome and the visited neighbour starts mocking until the visitors become an object of scorn, a constant humiliation with such an inescapable truth.

HE SPENT HIS FRIDAY nights smoking, and waiting for the next day to live again escaping his misery. One of his friends approached him with a business idea. A local house's owner had visited other relatives, so the place was an easy hit and no risk, a good place for the black market.

They all agreed to meet up later that night and one of the organisers brought a pickup truck to load the loot. Neil left Tammy worried after telling her that he'd found a piece job that evening. She could see through him that he was up to no good. For many nights, he wouldn't tell her anything, but to come back the next morning with a lame excuse for the previous night.

Hours passed away as they waited impatiently to do the job. Around half past one midnight, a group of young people and few elderlies gathered. They drove off in two trucks. Around two in the morning, they were collecting things out of the house. One of the individuals involved had known the family for some time and he was fully aware of the alarm systems.

They switched off the electricity from the meter box and started using torch lights silently. Successfully, they carried expensive furniture, and electronic gadgets of all kind. They drove in hot pursuit avoiding any glares from local residents. It took them a three-kilometre drive from that house to the warehouse.

> Usually, when slavery is repeated, it finds peaceful people and turns them into cruel revenge seeking murderers, only a few are saved from it. When people are freed from slavery, their humanity is changed in terms of thoughts. These are permutations taking place in the non-physical world.

They reached the rented warehouse and unloaded all the property into it. After unloading the loot, they drove back to their homes. Two weeks passed as they were busy selling off the loot at a very low price. They did split the money among seven people and unfairly as usual. Neil received his share and bought home groceries.

His mother kept telling him how unhappy she was whenever he was out there doing drugs. She would warn him about the consequences of foolishness, but he was not wise before experience and nothing else would penetrate into his thick skull. Whenever he brought groceries home, she would thank God, but inside of her, she was discerning that something wicked was going to happen to her son, although he was just trying to be a man of the house.

"My child do not go along with them! Stay far away from their paths, they rush to commit robbery. If a bird sees a trap being set, it knows to stay away. These people set an ambush for themselves and they are trying to get themselves killed. Such is the fate of all who are greedy for money, it robs them of life," she said this quoting from the book of proverbs. However, her hopes in him were as strong as a rock, come wind through thunder.

> It is like during those days when we go through bad times and promise ourselves never to hurt others like how we were hurt before, but most of the times, we hurt others worse aftermath. This world is not developing progressively, but we are in a world of capitalist mentality, the child laborer, a decline in marriages and isolation of families.

Moreover, as a mother she could not give up, it was like her strength had been renewed. It is nearly impossible to redeem a soul that needs no redemption. She could see where this was clearly heading. Her other daughter had just become a single mother of two children with different fathers. Such is common for a woman focused on her outside beauty, without anything of intellectual value buried in her skull, and following glamorous fashion trends all her life.

Neil's Mother was talking to him one evening after his daily routines.

She said, "My child, life is too short to take chances with it and whoever loves instruction, loves knowledge but who hates correction is stupid." Her words were driven from Solomon's wisdom and she blamed herself for Neil's unprecedented behaviour.

> However, young males living in the streets have enough energy that needs to be utilized either in the military or in infrastructures. If this energy is not used at all, it affects a great mass and it is a recipe for crimes. For a young woman, before she is twenty-five years old, she has three children and unmarried. Sex and drugs become the only entertainment.

After their first robbery, many break-ins followed, this remained unique because someone was always notifying them which house to hit. They had loaded guns. Night after night they consulted together, but they could not think of any better feasible scheme.

The man whose house was robbed paid a private investigator to open ears and eyes, from the results of it, the investigator performed well. He was tipped off from one snitch to another.

TWO MONTHS PASSED AFTER Neil and others had done the first robbery. The investigation had come to light as one of the accused started blaming and condemning others. One thief was promised to walk away free by compromising others, but it took threats and physical assaults to give out names.

He could not hold it back anymore, so he gave them names of those who were less threatening in the crew. Two police vehicles started collecting them one by one. Neil was the third in rank of Smalls and Kabelo cuffed in the vehicle. Suddenly, two men in casual clothing knocked on the door. Neil's mother walked to the door, "who might it be? Maybe one of the next door neighbours," she thought. Neil was at the back yard smoking.

Same social problems are everywhere including in Europe, America, Asia, Africa and Australia, this problem perseveres, it is worse after sending such people into prison in an effort for them to change. They are forced to face the reality of poverty, the only option is turning into petty thieves and prostitutes. They end up spending youth moments in condescension.

Hello, Mama," one of the cops at the door greeted her.

She replied, "how are you?

They told her everything was fine, but although she remained nervous.

She asked, "is there something wrong? And who are you two by the way? She only had a glimpse of the storyline. She could not argue with them any further after they had told her about their intruded sudden visit. This hurt her so much. Neil had finished his joint.

His mother stood outside her door helpless and staring with her tearing eyes when they cuffed him. And took her son away. His pregnant girlfriend also was left broken-hearted and humiliated. She could not take it anymore and went inside of the house and started packing whatever she had. Her life with Neil had been struck with a bolt of dark lightning.

"My life away from him is better than this," she thought. Abortion was not an option. The thought of it tormented her, she feared it so much.

Neil was surprised to see Smalls and Kabelo in the vehicle, they couldn't say anything to each other, but questions and hatred rose. They didn't trust each other at all. After all, whatever they'd used to cover their faces did not help them to hide their true identities.

More prisons are built and developed over these issues. Education is for the privileged. Many after serving their time in prison, the situations are bad and worse outside, mostly they have children to take care of. A society cannot be built based on punishment. Punishment and pain are a small thing to a giant in the end.

They picked up the fourth and last person, Mad kora. They were all taken to the police station for further investigation. Unfortunately, they were placed in different cells to avoid continuous fights.

Neil was angry, confused and unfocused. When he did all the robbery, he wouldn't understand about further consequences. Tammy had millions of thoughts crucifying her, "is it worth to interfere with such a person? Her life was built on mistakes and bad decisions.

Chicanery leadership displays total irresponsibility and incapability to handle the power of any sort, leaving a hopeless imbalanced and confused society. Not of less consideration was the fact that we are in the view of so many barbarous nations, who esteem and extol him who conquers.

An enemy's roots are bonded with his opponent's; it is then worthless to prone the leaves only. Roots must be carefully trimmed and during that process an opponent has to trim his own roots also, to completely plant a new seed of life. We have a hybrid of seeds, which means lemon trees are producing oranges. Since the beginning of civilization, people were living under certain rules and regulations. Education was used in writing and sending messages. The education and motivation behind capitalist based mentality reduce human consciousness development.

Rest assure that knowledge is important, nevertheless, educating people about how to be better individuals is a lost chapter in this life we are living today. Possibilities that comes from acquiring knowledge are countless as they improve a day to day life. A single person seeks to control a certain area to earn power, a legacy is not created and power is poison in the wrong hands. Education in Africa does not cater to its needs because of the motivation behind it. Most have abandoned the system only leaving it to those privileged enough to continue, and they grow up to become control freaks of the next generation.

PEOPLE EAT RAT POISON and expect not to die from it. Most of us easily fall for envy and jealousies among friends. Through everything, from pain to grievance, forgiveness is hard and the damage is huge. Colonization is a manipulation to serve one's best interest, and that oppression leads to wars. Peace, love, and joy are everything. Education starts in the family. Youth is not as lost as those before them, as usual, an apple doesn't fall away from the tree. Engineers should educate for a better tomorrow through actions.

Chapter 02 - Christina's Dilemma

THE FORMER DETECTIVE's death had become the centre of arguments. The new female investigator brought in to handle the matter remained focused with an ambition to get justice to all these victims. She was tired of playing politics, watching families ripped apart and the poorer getting more oppressed as the laws of a state always serve the interest of a ruling class.

After all this time, she figured out that a man called George had several answers to her questions, but he was hard to find like a ghost that comes on its terms. She had nothing on her plate for him to chew on, so he avoided meeting up with her. Otherwise, he had no idea if she was trustworthy, in this particular situation none of this investigation showed progress.

> WHEN A COUNTRY'S ECONOMY is like a rose trampled on the ground, Prisons are filled with people younger than thirty years. Two groups of social classes are built and funded, the rich and the poor. The middle class barely exist, and an individual becomes a nomad who moves beyond borders for greener pastures.

However, the investigation escalated to some dedicated members of justice. When they started uncovering hidden skeletons many were dirty and filthy as mud. When this was discovered many paid off their crimes by money, and again the dirt was swept under the carpets.

The female investigator kept pursuing deep into the truth. Issues were adding up further into a puzzle. People that she had long suspected seemed as they'd nothing to do with the killings. Mostly these customers and suppliers were in political and corporation power.

A retired former police minister was responsible for all these damages. This former minister and others in power carried cruelty against those that had different opinions related to greed and corruption.

THE FEMALE DETECTIVE WAS stuck to see her investigation through due to a lack of evidence, but she remembered turning down another young officer who persistently offered her a helping hand several times. Yet, she refused for obvious reasons and she thought of his interest, in this case, was driven by a certain objective different from hers, pertaining to what she had stood for. Typically, in her desperate moments, he approached her to help out again and this time she couldn't deny him but to go with it.

> Human subconscious development is true education. History has provided the same corrupt leadership without the knowledge to lead, so they just follow the sheep. WE LIVE IN A WORLD with an old judiciary system that is more three thousand years old, it has existed in full power.

Take a sit," she said, "I have a certain code for you to work on this case."

He interrupted, "what is this code?

"The first one is; do not interrupt me before I am done speaking. The second one is; we are not partners. You report to me and I do not report to you, last but not least, whatever we find in this case stays between me and you until proven true." She gave him orders.

She told him that the case had traitors within, and nobody could be trusted. The former minister made her furious.

The young officer encouraged Christina, "two heads are better than one and after the darkest night always comes a brighter day." She then believed they could be trust between them. The Former Detective had placed the young officer on a spotlight and he was not just another officer, but he showed potential and courage in many cases. Christina longsighted the same thing in him, it was the right time to create a team inspired by justice, not by fear.

> What is the difference in our laws, when lawmakers are masters of the law instead of servants? Peace is hard to come by when ignorance is bliss. Judgment is upon every wicked man until this world stops persecuting innocent people for the well-heeled.

Weeks had passed since Christina and Melvin had started working together. They were gathering the evidence, so that, they could have a strong case to bring down a very powerful corrupt man. This man had other men in his pockets, many people that surrounded Christina and Melvin were involved in this investigation. Proud, both from adulation and native disposition, Marvin yet was polite and affable.

One of the people who had his name linked to this turned out that he had predicted his own death, he left the police work for a while when corruption had increased amongst police officers. He watched police officers raping and killing women, from that day he stopped taking orders and all his political views changed. Many became scared that he was going to spit the beans and they could not risk the exposure.

Another Politician warned his wife about government officials' involvement in dirty deals, but she couldn't do anything. He was shot at a red robot. His wife and children were at the back seat of a vehicle. The incident took place a few metres from their home. Two men wearing big jackets approached the vehicle holding huge guns ready to fire.

> It is only possible when a nation is separated that corruption erupts like a volcano to the point that it is unstoppable. The emphasis on tertiary education is overlooked. A major bias in tertiary education in that many people if not everyone, goes to school for a better income in the near future.

They did shoot him a couple of times. And some fired shots missed the wife at the back seat. She did not scream, only tears wear crawling out of her fearful eyes. The wife and children survived the ruthless wrath.

His destiny ended up in a ditch because of his different opinion in politics, the news went viral and fear increased among the remained politician.

George had a list of politicians who had dirty money, a spoil alert, they were using it to smuggle guns for their own protection.

Although, these two officers wanted a team so much they were forced never to trust anyone else besides the two of them. Their last option was to join into the corruption and destroy it from the inside-out.

CHRISTINA AND MARVIN were enjoying a political drama, whilst waiting for George to give them information to make right moves and arrests. Although, it was not helping them enough as they were looking at a criminal rampage. George wanted Christina to clear all his criminal record in an exchange with information.

George wanted to be set free from the police's most wanted billboard, and he paid judges to set aside some of his crimes. What he couldn't clear was his own conscience, which was filled with pictures of shame and disappointments.

> When the time comes for them to use their youthful advantage, they are then trapped with modern day slavery, working for promotion. Education is still missing in our homes, and people tend to confuse learning a profession for education.
> If so, they are trapped from the beginning to set goals throughout. Machines are increasing and taking away the so-called 'jobs', by installing a computer program many jobs are wiped off in the modern day working industry. It motivates wars and discourages peace.

A former detective's death came out of George's selfish motives. George told these two young officers, Christina and Melvin to stand aside as individuals were killing each other in a game of loyalty. The city newspaper in the weeks that followed published articles about a Mayor who was incarcerated inside of his house after some things were discovered. The judges were paid off. The mayor walked away a free man.

George gave them a list of names, and a piece of advice, either, to continue with it at the cost of their families or to quit. Most of the time, they spent cleaning up crimes, but that was not even close to real duty. They looked for only a small percentage that was either clean or not involved at all. More than an expected number of the force officers cheats and steals from the same people they are supposed to protect.

Basically, those who can afford better education are totally different from those that are poor to do so, yet we are reminded that education offers equal opportunities. People from poor lives should focus less on receiving the so-called 'education' and improve entrepreneurial skills, in most cases, they have nothing to lose.

Almost seventy-five percent of people in Africa are highly talented, but they are persuaded into professions required in America, Europe, and Asia. Africa was not colonised over education failure, it was an adding factor. African countries were colonized out of greedy, and this greedy long started with indigenous chiefs.
Tribal leaders sold other people into foreign lands for guns. It was not a situation where people were not educated. Chiefs saw an opportunity to increase tribal strength, and that did not go well at the end.

The same nature is still around, being the reason that sixty years later after freedom the continent has an increase in poverty. Governments are ignorant about the needs of people. The propaganda on colonization and decolonization is discussed repeatedly. The greatest minds in the African leadership forums think for themselves.
We cannot discuss old wars while ignoring modern battles, the future is here. African Union is a failed organization. They have accepted donations from corrupt leaders, whose countries are in jeopardy, suffering from high unemployment rates.

During the last days of Leader Gaddafi, NATO intervened with the African affairs, allegedly destroying Libya water pipes claiming about weapons hidden in these pipes, the familiar strategy destroyed Iraq. The organization that represents the Africans is a double-edged shape knife then, we are forced to listen when they preach stories of wars.

The world is not based on color superiority, and color does not rule the world, trades do. The love of money is the root of all evil, the war in this world is between the poor and the rich.

We are forced to support evil people because of power and money. The continent is not improving in trades even if people have acquired education later after colonisation. Unity is the first improvement. The only way we can make a distinction is to put our differences aside and start focusing on one state that provides food, security, clothing, and water, above all love. African leaders are blaming Europeans, Chinese and Americans for their own failures. When we do not close the doors, we create a playground for exploitation.

AT THE FOUNDATION OF CONFUCIUS' thought was that a society existed in different times, i.e., the feudal structure as it had developed during the decadence of the Chou kingdom; the men to whom he addressed himself were the gentlemen. He accepted this society and within its frame tried to build up a conservative polity based on a high moral standard.

A man ought to act in society, not for any profit, but only because he thinks it's right and proper, and therefore morally obligatory, to act in a given manner, even if his action cannot be crowned by success. It follows from this that righteousness is the leading idea of the political man. This is nothing close to what an African political man is. They have a tendency of living above the law.

Chapter 03 - Mother's burden

Neil's mother was there through the badlands and court procedures, hoping that the justice system would find him innocent. The bail was raised much higher than she could imagine, she only cried in tears to God looking for answers.

She said to him, "My child if you listen well to me one last time, your journey shall be loosened up."

She bought a Holy Bible and another book to read, "Do not reject discipline; you will only make it hard for yourself. Understanding and wisdom shall grow within you."

His mother encouraged him, "this is your time to learn from previous mistakes and correct them on the way. Think about your life and what kind of a father you want to be? And what you want most."

She held his hands while praying and hoping for the best. She could only offer a prayer for a clemency outcome.

She visited him as much as she could remember, but although he missed Tammy more than others, she never visited. Still, the more he thought about her, the more he understood about serving time.

To assuage his misery he betook himself to study and the composition of music and poetry. Another thing that constantly nagged him were these warnings from his mother; "STOP PLAYING WITH FIRE."

Politicians will keep on repeating the same mistakes using other people. It is just a matter of time, but somewhere soon slavery will happen in the same way it happened several years ago. Migrants from Nigeria suffer torments in Libya. Africans used to avoid massacres through FREE MOVEMENT.

He took out some books and started reading them, but it was a privilege sometimes to actually contemplate on what he was doing because of noise. His cell had another young man of the same age. Both of them wanted to leave the dungeon and focus on life. They talked about old wonders and most of their stories were related. They became friends.

Furthermore, one thing that influenced and inspired his whole life was rap music. His new friend Mhazi Chuma well known as Spila had a thing for music also. Mhazi never had any privileges of life, so to make a living he started stealing cars. He had familiarized himself with street life.

In a way, they started spending time freestyling without a beat and making up rhymes. Other young prisoners gathered around listening to them. They wrote rhymes, love poems and even short stories based on the ghetto struggles.

ON THE OTHER HAND, Jadea was lost in the wilderness while searching for a locked-up convict. He was lucky to find Tanya's trace, whose life was trapped in a tunnel of crack. Crystalmeth had deteriorated his health and he spent most of his time heavily medicated. And money problems increased as the addiction had increased.

Human nature is becoming increasingly incompetent as we focus on our financial wellbeing. Parents should teach children love, peace, and unity because we are running out of these things, yet again gaining all the material things the world can offer could be nothing when the soul is empty and deranged.

Jadea made his research well. He finally ran into him after asking around. All these terrible changes did not mean that he was forgiven. Jadea had found another imprisoned youth.

He talked to him and gave him a ziplock bag with meth. They went into Jadea's car. It was not as fancy as the one he had before. Instead of beating him up for answers and the whereabouts of his old friend, he gave him meth to make it easier.

Surely, Tanya was in a condition to accept anything for his drug addiction. Jadea knew the young man would open up like a highway at four in the morning.

His simple idea worked and he asked, "you are the one who shot me right?

"No, No," he answered petrified.

"Neil was the one who shot you, not me." He told him everything that Foster put them through and how they had figure out that money was the roots of all this. They both laughed like friends, and Tanya kept on speaking.

"Where is your other friend, who shot me? Jadea asked.

"Last time I heard, they say he is serving a two year sentence on a correctional facility for theft," Tanya replied.

Jadea's spirit broke, but his effort for revenge strengthened him again as the little bird kept on opening up. Questions after questions, he kept on asking.

Tanya whispered, "He stole your car and sold it." He then gave up Neil's house address. Jadea walked away living Tanya reflecting on what he had just said for a few stones.

WHILST, NEIL WAS STILL struggling to put rhyming words together because of poor vocabulary, Mhazi kept on encouraging him to read more. And Mhazi never had any visits. Neil sounded like one of his old favorite hip hop artists. They were inspired to do more writing and reading. He wrote using the third-person omniscient point of view.

> People in this world have nothing against each other, but those that are in power, to remain in power they usually manipulate those without power to separate, with hatred and racism opinions. A man whose leadership only empowers him is blind and his flock is lost as well.

None of his relatives and friends visited him except for his mother. He was now used to the situation and tried to make the best out of it. Nobody can get used to living behind bars, but it only becomes familiar with time. He took all these emotions and tried to put them down to create a record, and failure kept him going. This emerged as a new world to him, they'd the freedom of music and his mother brought music CDs on her most visits.

ALL THIS WAS NOT making him a better individual on the contrary. His literature and music was a portrait of himself. Some people were smuggling cigarettes and marijuana on an elevated cost due to the correctional facility's economy and trading rates.

He thought of it as his chance to quit. He was not getting any special treatment like other gangs because he was not in any gang. Two gangs, 26s, and 28s had a pitiless rivalry between them. He didn't want to be part of it, but surviving as an independent individual meant keeping your head down.

The only way for a dictator to rule is only if the country is divided. When a country is divided into many fractions, it is nearly impossible to collaborate understanding, and the reason being those leaders in small fractions have different agendas for the people that they are actually leading.

JADEA ONCE AGAIN made his next move, he visited the exact place that Tanya had told him. On his arrival, he expected to see Neil and catch him while asleep at service. Prison in another way had protected Neil from a terrific and bad fate. Neil was only used to his Mother's visits that Jadea surprised him.

When he saw Jadea, he could not recognize him at first, they robbed him at night. He thought, "Maybe this is the man to bail me out".

"Do you remember me," Jadea asked.

"No, remind me again," Neil replied. Jadea laughed that instant, it was a total surprise to him.

"Young man, you shot me and took my car," Jadea said. Neil said nothing at first. He looked into Jadea's eyes without fear. They had a grudge between them. Actually, there was no need to fear him because of the prison bars, although Jadea did not visit to play mind games, this was serious business.

"Long time," Jadea said, "what are you in here for? Let me guess, probably another robbery."

"Not very well since I have been locked up here," Neil replied, "I am sure, you did not come all the way to address me about my life, please cut to the chase."

Quickly Jadea replied, "I am here for my car and money."

Neil's voiced out, "I do not know what you are talking about."

"If you do not have both of these things, then what should I do with you, young man? Then give me an offer I cannot refuse, maybe I will not crucify you on a wall."

Neil replied, "I wish to do something for you, but these walls limit my lucrative businesses."

"All the things you stole from me cost about two hundred and fifty thousand, being here is not a reason," Jadea said, "Expect me in two weeks."

NEIL WAS TRAUMATIZED BECAUSE THE threats were as real as the bars he was living in. Jadea did not seem threatened but his words left a soul petrified. He remained persistent with his suppose revenge idea, he saw an opportunity in an ambitious young man whose spirit is like that of a hunting lion. The following week Jadea came back and gave Neil a way out.

Neil's mother tried to put money together, but that was not helping at all. She had a struggle talking to some family members for contribution.

> Some people need power in order to exploit others. History will be repeated and eyes will not see it, neither will ears hear it. In Africa, we tend to search for investors before we create an environment to invest.

Afterward, Jadea said, 'I have people in positions and in few weeks you will walk out of here clean like nothing ever happened." Neil was happy after Jadea had promised him freedom, the part he did not well understand was that Jadea had an end goal after all. Neil desperately wanted to get out this situation, he was willing to accept a rotten fish for supper just to be out of prison.

Jadea asserted, "you will do what I say and when I say it, in that way, you will be able to pay me back."

Neil said, "I shot you under certain orders to retrieve the package." He then told him they would meet for further business.

Neil spent the rest of that day excited. He spoke about it to other prisoners and not everybody was happy for him. He thought that leaving prison and back into the world would bring him a new life and another chance to face his problems fearlessly. He bragged to a point that one of the inmates broke out a fight with him.

ABOUT TWO WEEKS AFTER Jadea had told him about getting out earlier than expected, another fight broke out in the toilets and Neil stabbed his opponent in self-defence.

> A garden can have many crops, but bad crops are thrown into a fire when we assume that adding fertilizer to a bad seed will help us harvest more, we are much likely to harvest nothing. It is more alike when we expect a bad tree to bear good fruits, and with such high expectations, we are likely to die of hunger.

Jadea's words were like an early Christmas miracle for Neil's bondages, the judge only said he had served enough of his sentence. Neil had no idea about the way Jadea took care of it, and it mattered not, because what was important for him was to be a free man.

Finally, the walls were out of his path. He wanted to go home to his mother. Too broke and embarrassed to show up, six months had passed and that felt almost like a year.

Neil embraced his pride and went home thinking about the right words for a right apology. He kept on breaking her heart after she had tried her best in raising him. He knocked on the door, and she was not home. Weeks before he got out of prison, his child was born. He had many plans for his new founded life and the future of his child crossed his mind.

Selfishness satisfies its own needs. Life behind a desk is better than living through other people's pain. Generally, after many people graduate with high hopes of huge incomes and promotions, they are faced with financial stress later in life.

When it comes to current education, it will never offer students reality and the actual truth about the modern economy, and that is the power of free innovations. We can only accomplish many things if we educate ourselves, rather than when we are educated by a failed system. When education is practical, students learn, observe and act on problems in society.

He took a walk around the city looking for his old mates. Although, he avoided visiting some of them. Community elders were not interested in his negative impact. Nevertheless, great joy kept him going up and down the streets. Nothing had changed at all. Drunkards were still wasting away money on liquor. They were all still struggling to buy one bottle of alcohol.

He thought, 'maybe I am over thinking about everything, it is just that I haven't been around for a while.' He murmured, "I'm free now".

His old friends were smoking sitting in an old cabin, so they invited him in. They were all smoking in rounds. They screamed for him with joy, they'd respect for ex-prisoners. He asked one of his old friends a question, "do you know about any studio around here that can do music demos?

One of the people replied, "I heard that Smash is cooking some dope entertainment, maybe you should try him. After months of bars, you are a rapper now."

They joked and laughed about it together as if he was not serious about it.

We live in a society that knows nothing about long term investment, and a society that is educated for employment. Fear of failure is a reason for poverty, not education. Fear of change, fear of risky and fear of tomorrow, so in this way, we will never know what is living for the moment.

AFTER THEY HAD SMOKED, he went back home to check if his mother was back. She was totally surprised while preparing for another visit, and she had not given up. A mother's caring heart could not let go.

Neil and his mother were rejoicing. With tears of joy in her eyes, she cooked good food and sat down to eat with her son.

The food tasted delicious, he ate while rejoicing. She had cooked the food with her whole heart, and Neil had not eaten such tasty food in a very long time. When she saw the empty plate, she smiled and said, "Wauya Kumba mwanangu."

She wanted to ask about the sudden release, but happiness had overwhelmed her. Remembering the past is painful and carrying it around is work overload. When he heard about his child, the excitement increased, and quietly, it was like he never suggested an abomination abortion before. Such thoughts were always in his blood, but fear is stupidity in the eyes of cowards.

He took a shower and changed his clothes, he smelled good compared to the acrid prison hanging odour. He had some money stored in his old snickers. He took it out and used it to buy some few things. He bought some baby diapers and a small blue bear.

For all of this, the money was still not enough. He went to one of his old crew members, especially those that would fall for original snickers on a very low price. His thoughts only wanted to go and see his baby with whatever he had.

He boarded a bus to a place where Tammy was living. It was a long cruise for a person who wanted to be there fast. Neil the first time he looked at his own son had a breath of eagerness, and composure for a second left his body. From these innocent eyes, he decided to be a man and a father, but not a husband. He knew his absence had created tensions between him and Tammy. He kissed the little one on the forehead and promised to come back very soon to care of him.

It is tiring to work in a world where ethics do not exist. A gangster wears a police uniform and carries around licensed guns. The government serves the people, not the other way around. It is like whoever is destined for leadership is also destined for evil deeds.

Jadea for some time remained out of the picture waiting for the right time to start using Neil. He took a bus again and sat down back in a corner. His fears were his strength and motivation to accomplish anything at any given time. His pressure was to put food on the table.

Life is a path and it leads to many destinations. Money and fame are just an illusion of a desperate thought. Hustling is a dominant thought, and slowly, he could not shake off these thoughts out of his mind.

Neil's interest in music could actually make up for his father's lost time and covers old scars. Pursuing a goal is to accomplish it. 'Rap is a style and a skill.'

It was bad enough that whatever they were going to do to earn a living was out of desperate thoughts, and in his conscious mind, going back to prison was unexpected.

It was time for Neil Hadebe to put his child's future first. He had a job interview, and getting that job would enable him to provide for his son and his mother. Jadea had a way for Neil to make money full time, but it was illegal. Going back to school was too much of a responsibility for a young hustler.

NEIL ARRIVED HOME around seven at night, and fortunately, he had a visitor that his mother had prepared some food for. He opened the door and found Jadea waiting for him. He had already told Neil's mother that he was behind the release of her boy, in this way she treated him like family. Jadea was a gangster and Neil knew this. "Come and eat with us, Jadea was just telling me how you two met," Neil's mother said.

He replied, "Oh, did he." He joined them and remained silent while these two exchanged words and food dishes. They had a good meal, and then Jadea had his goodbyes. Neil's mother remained behind cleaning up the table whilst Neil walked the man out to his vehicle.

It is true that power in great percentages is always in the wrong hands. People vote power to the leader including rights to live. Typically, a person who smokes a cigarette is a victim of it and one cannot damage a cigarette by smoking it. We speak of what we heard, read and gained confidence while misinformed.

"You have a new car now," Neil said.

" Of course, your mother she is a very nice person, I hope to visit her sometime," Jadea laughed, "I have this new job coming up and you have to come on board," he added.

Neil replied, "I thank you for what you did for me, but this life of crime is not the way for me. I'm leaving it behind to take care of my life."

"So you thought after I got you out using my money and not forgetting that you still owe me, you want to be holy out here, I will leave you to think about it overnight and make sure that it is the right decision," Jadea said this and drove off.

> CORRUPTION IS LIKE EBOLA and Ebola is easily transmitted. A virus that the corrupt system carries is a burden to the whole body. From 1983 to 1987, a genocide happened in Zimbabwe over a mixture of politics and tribalism. Another Rwanda Genocide killed hundreds of thousands because of political and tribal issues.

> Hiroshima and Nagasaki - Apocalyptic Reality of Japan, last but not least religious beliefs wars are causing an infanticide in the mid-east. Africa has an increase in terrorism from particular groups as all this is caused by one particular problem and that is a misunderstanding between nations, politicians, and citizens.

Neil spends the whole night thinking of what could have or what should have been and what it should be. His way out was cornered but as always there is another choice. He had a sleepless night over thoughts and choices; he woke up to smoke on two different occasions. Closely paying attention to any of it would best serve him. Nothing belonged to him, until he had learned to overtake all his challenges and do what he never did before, easy money was a way to go, but that also had consequences.

His child needed a father and his drug addiction needed to stop at some point. Most of those that grew up with him wouldn't help him, for they couldn't overcome a bottle of cough syrup that had ruined their lives. Neil felt the need to change his character, yet he did what he hated most and then gave a reason contradicting his behaviour.

Anyway, this Jadea person only wanted the best for him, he had helped him to get out of jail on a clean sheet. Even if he was going to get a job, it was nothing close to what Jadea wanted for him. Cooking for a minimum wage was never going to get him going on the same road with Jadea.

He made a decision that morning, "nothing would ever go wrong," he thought. He went back to sleep with a straight determined mind. His mother made a prayer and it seemed the more she wanted the best for him, only evil kept knocking at her door. Neil fell asleep around three in the morning, the world gave him choices to make and prison had provided the required discipline to do so.

Early morning, Neil took out a card that had Jadea's number on it and called him. They talked for about two minutes and that was enough for them to arrange an meeting afternoon. He made the call at six in the morning. He went to take a bath and put on his clothes.

Confusion and ignorance are enemies of faith and belief. Obedient plays a radical part during the change of a heart and commitment is stronger when words are fulfilled by action. The political error in the African society is that no-one is guilty to be arrested of a certain crime.

A guilt person usually walks away because of money and strong relations. A new world of technology is a new age where information is expensive and the press is a powerful weapon. Freedom is an outreach; we are granted independence to live as if we are owned from birth because at times we are. Even one of the richest country in the world poor people are found within its streets and corners.

When his mother saw him that morning, she was as excited as she was the day she gave birth to him. Neil started living a double life, and he looked in the mirror and saw his father in him wearing formal clothing.

Since this is what he chose to do, studios were at hand and if they would do a good job, he was going to be able to afford his equipment, and start recording his music. He was away from all these girls for the past six months, he thought to sleep with one of his ex-girlfriends as a good start. An old snake with a new skin, yet, he remembered, "if it was not for that snitch, he would be somewhere in life." Anger rose and forgiveness fled away from his heart.

For the wrath of God is revealed from heaven against all ungodliness and unrighteousness of men, who suppress the truth in righteousness, because what may be known of God is (a) manifest in them, for God has shown it to them. Forever since the world was created, people have seen the earth and sky. Through everything God made, they can clearly see his obscure qualities, eternal power, and divine nature. So they have no excuse for not knowing God. Yes, they knew God. But they wouldn't worship him as God or even give him thanks. And they began to think up foolish ideas of what God was like. As a result, their minds became dark and confused.

Claiming to be wise, they instead became utter fools. And instead of worshiping the glorious, ever-living God, they worshiped idols made to look like mere people and birds and animals and reptiles. SO GOD ABANDONED THEM to do whatever shameful things their hearts desired. As a result, they did vile and degrading things with each other's bodies. They traded the truth about God for a lie. They worshiped and served the materials God created instead of the creator himself, who is worthy of eternal praise! Amen. That is why God abandoned them to their shameful desires. For even their woman exchanged the natural use for what is against nature.

Likewise, also the men, leaving the natural use of the woman, burned in their lust for one another, men with men committing what is shameful, and receiving in themselves the penalty of their error which was due. Since they thought it foolish to acknowledge God, He abandoned them to their foolish thinking and let them do things that should never be done. Their lives became full of every kind of wickedness, sin, greed, hate, envy, murder, quarreling deception, malicious behaviour, and gossip. They are backstabbers, haters of God, insolent, proud, and boastful.

They invent new ways of sinning, and they disobey their parents. They refuse to understand, break their promises, are heartless, and have no mercy. They know God's justice requires that those who do these things deserve to die, yet they do them anyway. Worse yet, they encourage others to do them, too. You may think you can condemn such people, but you are just as bad, and you have no excuse! When you say they are wicked and should be punished, you are condemning yourself, for you who judge others do these very same things.

Chapter 04 - A Not-So-Good Person

THE FIRST DAY, HE WENT looking for work and everything went perfect, he took out his curriculum vitae. He carried a bunch of files with him and went into central business district to look for a job. It was around eight in the morning, by that time, he wanted to catch small new business shops before business hours.

Most of his old friends were still sleeping during that time. He walked from one shop to another looking for a job, in each one of these shops they referred him onto the next. Luckily, he was patient enough until one man asked him to come in for an interview. They talked and understood each other, although the young man was not happy with the final pay negotiation.

> MOST PEOPLE GET STUCK looking for a different type of encouragement than the one they have already, they are bound to make wrong decisions. Some do not think about the decisions. In this life, there is a stage that once a door is opened for one person, it is either the person answers or totally ignores because of what they might be doing during that certain time.

His new employer told him the following day was the best for him to start. He took a taxi back home and one of his ex-girlfriends was desperate to sleep with him as well. He had been from a correctional facility, and that gave him a biased reputation in the streets.

It was around eleven in the morning when he took a few bucks and bought a bottle of wine. She was home alone that time and music was loud.

Hours passed, Neil headed to another golf club that they'd agreed to meet with Jadea and he arrived there earlier than expected. He actually found Jadea in a bar, sitting on a table alone. When Neil walked in to join him, a waiter approached the table.

"How are you two gentlemen doing today? A waiter asked. "Fine man, please your strongest whiskey on blocks. Make it two please," Jadea replied.

They sat down and ordered food, and their whiskey orders were brought on the table instantly. They ordered some ribs and tossed their glasses to business and success.

Pick friends carefully because demons exist as well as Angels. The world does not change, or does it pursue any change in morals. The meaning of life is a lesson taught by few and only enforced by many. Knowledge is like a key that either lives the door open or closes the door for a fool.

Everything starts small, a journey of a thousand miles starts with one step and even a book of a thousand words start with a letter.

The food was delicious and they both enjoyed it. Jadea picked up a brown bag that was on the floor and gave it to Neil. He took out a paper, pen and wrote an address, and a person's name to deliver the package to. He gave it to Neil and told him to make the delivery the following day in the evening. "I will get to you as soon as the delivery has been made." Neil took that package, he wanted to ask what it was, but he was in a difficult position to ask questions.

They went separate ways and Neil went straight home, where his mother was waiting for him. She eagerly waited to hear about the interviews. She was working from seven to five. At around five, he arrived home carrying his backpack.

He went home and sat with his mother while she was cooking. She had already missed him so much, it was clear to see from her eyes. He avoided spoiling her joy by getting involved with gangs again. Her heart was proud to see him doing something for a change. Neil's other relatives had visited after they heard about his release from prison.

His sister came through among those that had visited. Although she was still angry with him, it all faded away after she saw him. As siblings, she did not buy the "changed man" thing, however, she believed him.

Prison is something that changes a person forever. People are condemned by idols they follow. Young people should know that trends like fashion, music and other glamorous fruits started ages ago. It is the very reason why many young girls are not graduating into adults; life is cut short after falling pregnant.

The dinner went well until someone knocked on the door.

"Don't worry, I will get it," Neil shouted. When he opened the door, he saw a man that he used to work for before the arrest standing there with a crocodile smile.

"Hello, so after you get out of prison, you do not come and greet your elders, but that matters not because we are still here for you," the tall, slim and dark man who stood at the gate said this.

"They are three sides to every story man, what do you want," Neil replied.

"Okay, I see how you want to play, but I won't do that to you, I will always take care of you. That brings me to say there is a new job tonight and it's a big one. Trust me on this one, I won't let you go down alone," he added.

Neil replied, "I am done with everything I ever did for you.

Thank you for passing by."

Neil closed the gate and the tall gentlemen stood there angry.

The young man went back inside, his sister asked, "a friend of yours?

"Nah, wrong address," Neil replied. "Okay, if you say so!" She said. The night went well as usual after watching many television programs, they all went to sleep one after another.

> Money is not the only purpose for living like how this world domi-
> nators have painted the picture. Learn to live for others and inspire
> the person next to you. What you laugh at as funny or a joke is the
> truth that annoys ignorant people, yet it saves them from this world.

Early morning Neil woke up and took a warm bath for thirty minutes, he had not done such a thing for several months. He collected his bank papers to his new workplace. While wearing formal clothes. Unusual, he arrived at the place earlier than all other employees.

TWENTY MINUTES PASSED as he sat outside waiting for his employer to arrive. Soon as they'd arrived business started in the kitchen, a fast food restaurant. He knew absolutely nothing about cooking. They only employed him because he was willing to learn as fast as possible. He took his bag into a store and placed it underneath other bags. A day went-by selling fried chips and burgers.

Before afternoon, he'd asked for clock several times as if he was on medication. It was almost time to leave and attend his next 'real' business as he referred to it as.

They were no more customers walking in to buy food since they were all exhausted the restaurant closed earlier than usual. Neil finished his cleaning duties and hurried to make a delivery that came from Jadea.

He arrived at a place that was on the address and asked for the person that the delivery belonged to. The Security guard walked with him and left him on the door.

"Pox right! I have your package," Neil handed over the bag expecting some kind of payment in exchange.

> EDUCATION IS FOR EVERYONE dump, lame, crippled, blind, weak and strong, uncool and cool, irrelevant and relevant. If that system is only constructed in a way that some will never see the doors of it, then, what is the dream behind it?

The man looked inside of a brown bag and took the bag inside. "Thank you," he said. Neil left not sure if the exchange went well. Probably, Pox had a different discussion with Jadea.

Jadea phoned Neil so that they would have another meeting.

They picked up where they had left off the meeting. Jadea took out a couple of hundreds out of his pocket and gave them to Neil.

And Neil felt like he was working for something and that motivated him extensively. When he saw the money, he had goose bumps, it was a lot of money for doing something small.

Jadea gave him another brown bag and this time it was bigger than the previous bag. "Honesty is love and love is royalty, keep that in mind every time." Jadea wrote a name and the address on another small piece of paper.

The young man left and went home with the package, he realized that the deliveries were paying him a lot. He arrived home with few groceries.

Although he did not think through for a person who had just got a job. "Where did he get that money to buy all that stuff? His mother did not ask but she only hoped it had nothing to do with robbing houses. He had bought some stuff that belonged to his child, so he visited them that same evening.

Interestingly, they are several leaders that are very charismatic, yet very unwise because they implement ideas that they are not willing to participate in or even get involved to see them through. New or old leaders of many countries brought brilliant ideas on the table, yet their deeds were totally biased from the first go.

He arrived with a bag full of clothes, pampers and food for the baby. When Tammy saw him with all these groceries, she was impressed. She felt relieved from the burden of being a single mother. Just for a moment, she was stress-free from all the arguments they've had, even before Neil went to prison.

"I did not have this child by myself, you know," She would say it in tears. When Tammy saw Neil taking responsibility and accountability for his doings, she was overwhelmed by emotions.

However, he was the same person that once suggested an abortion, and Neil was prepared to be a better father, especially not after his father's footsteps. He left her some money to buy food and other things for their child.

Neil held his child closely, and kissed him on the forehead. He said, "Dad is going to take you with him."

Before he left, Tammy thanked him for coming through to see his child for the second time. However, Neil did not respond.

Gaddafi talked about unity and becoming one continent with free education at all levels, but that resulted differently. Consequences are terrifying when power is individualized, it forgets all the things that it can change and because of fear, all is ruined in an effort to protect that power.

AFTER ONE BUSY NIGHT, he woke up earlier than usual and prison had disciplined him well. He wore his work clothes and left to work in a rush hour. He went to buy something to smoke before turning up at work. Rush hour and a chill morning, every time he seemed over-dressed and it was not going along with the job and yet, it seemed like faith. Well outfitted, as if he was an office worker while he was spending the whole day cooking for minimum wages.

Whenever it was time to leave the house, he wore formally and carried his bag. Afterward, he left work early for another Jadea's client. Neil made the delivery as expected of him. Everything went well that day. This kept on going for days and those days changed into weeks and weeks into months. He took some of the money that Jadea was paying him and started working on an album.

AS MONTHS PASSED BY, he started spending more time in the studio to a point that his daily job became useless as far as he was concerned. After all, he once promised never to quit on something, but to earn something greater through hard work.

Soon as he started making that much, his loyal fan base grew rapidly and support in his shows improved. They charged a certain amount on the door into the club for a small percentage and all kinds of kids from different lives were coming in for a good show.

Life was sweet, the idea of going to school remained idle in Neil's mind. The more Jadea trusted Neil with all these brown bags it became clear that the business had grown. They were on top of their game. In those few months, Jadea bought another car, and Neil built his own studio and started recording his own music, while other artists were paying for a studio session.

Neil's eyes remained on the goal and just to improve in the rap game until it started paying the bills for him. His producer would drink syrup until he is almost colour-blind, but yet his production of beats and music was good. He still continued to extol his own calling in his songs, and was inclined to view with ridicule the unstable life of others.

> Institutions should be powerful enough to protect people from a violent leader and protect leaders from violent people. Leadership should rule based on the good of others, if that is not it, then rather stay in self-freedom than to be ruled by pure gangsters whose motives brings destruction.

The money from Jadea and deliveries made him a leader, he learned to be the shepherd and never the sheep in countless times. Neil Hadebe gathered his own team, some in marketing and some in product distribution.

His mother was always watching from a distance all these activities. Especially when he talked about his own production company that produces music and videos, hoping to expand into movies at some point. Jadea's deliveries did not stop because they were increasing the customer base.

Instead of making one delivery a night, they increased from five to twenty deliveries. Neil Hadebe made sure that they were no mistakes in deliveries, almost his life depended on them.

Jadea visited Neil's house and his mother a couple of times before they'd expanded. He told her that he had offered Neil a job at the office. Neil had worked and gained experience from Jadea. Everyone praised him for dressing well and that gave him a professional appearance.

Neil's mother at some point was impressed that finally, something good had emerged in her son's life.

Jadea gave Neil a gun to protect himself from there competitions. Neil picked up a gang that he started leading, at the same time, they all joined in for other private businesses with Jadea, and most of these businesses were illegal.

Life is made up of many elements, God is not religious and godliness is defined through a heart, not a religion. Jesus Christ of Nazareth taught many things that go beyond gender or anything that discriminates people from one another. People have different languages for a reason and different colors for a reason because beauty comes from different colors.

Neil remained the one to count stock from Jadea and to give it to his crew for different deliveries in different areas. All the payments were made through online banking systems. Jadea gave Neil money to pay the crew. The business became flawless like nothing else.

They said as long the music is good; it pushes you and itself into the market quicker than expected. He remained artistically vibrant and streetwise. Each one of those that worked with him also played a crucial role as part of the company. They stopped abusing hardcore drugs, and they focused on growing bigger each and every day.

As months were passing-by, Neil had nothing to prove until he was better than others, but surely with the amount of respect they were giving him, among them, he was the alpha.

Whenever he thought about it, he had finally become a leader and that terrified him most. They moved their music business into central business district permanently.

He could afford to keep his baby boy around, so he asked the baby mother to move in with him. They'd to start raising their own child together. Besides the fact that his mother persisted to see her grandchild more often.

Peace comes from different languages. People know the truth and mostly they hate it for different reasons due to different beliefs. When this truth is made out loud and clear, many are freed from the chains of this world. We forget the real reasons for this life because all the human focus is on problems that remain forever infinite one after another.

Light is grace and darkness is a part of this world. All of this is real when we chose to believe that it is.
A lie remains a lie no matter how different it is told, yet the truth remains the same as a thirst infant whose thirstiness can only be quenched by a mother's breastfeeding. A lie is a mother who quenches a child by a bottle of wine. She only corrupts the child permanently.

What kind of education people should consume? Entrepreneurship is totally a very different mindset. Life is not a race or some sort of competition because most people spend time trying to be extravagant or even more. It is not wrong to try all sorts of things, even when we are "fearful".

What comes first in this life is God, either one believes or does not believe, there is a Father, a Guardian, a Teacher and a Healer, God is the first in life but surprisingly fear is second and all other things such as religion and politics follow.
Capitalism is a system that seems as if it is motivating others to do better, but in other senses, some people do not recognize something within it. It is still the same system that has been used for ages to create a human god that the whole world can praise, and all wish to live under him.

There is a total difference between inspiration and an idol. It takes unity to build a structure and ideas from different heads to make up one big giant goal achievable by different means. People will not amount to anything unless they are taught how to do it. This makes a difference as many are learning the power of self-employment. It takes time to have innovated minds and a motivated personality, nothing is impossible under the sky. It all depends on one's point of view.

A person who goes to work every day knows the importance of work and that is the reason why they are never pushed to wake up from a bed and to become productive.

Chapter 05 - Moral Crossroads-Bad Behaviour

FURTHERMORE, IT WAS ANOTHER morning, after months had passed as Neil was still hustling through Jadea. He went to meet Jadea after they'd a meeting in the morning.

Jadea told Neil, "This thing is not bringing enough equity into our pockets. I have an inner city job for you and this one you do not have to involve some of your boys into it." "What is the job? Neil asked.

"Just know that it is a million-dollar job on the line here before you say yes, think deeply," Jadea responded.

> A fool quits because it is hard, however, there is no other replacement for hard work. Either face the fears and defeat them or suffer because of them. People are equipped to conquer their challenges. Those who succeed and oppress others they use fears as strength. Yet, they keep one entertained while they are at work.

Neil understood the risk of the job, it was a chance for him to have enough money to invest and boost his business. The love of money pulled him in. Neil knew that he had to be careful with his answer after Jadea's proposal. Jadea would never take "no" for an answer. He only gave Neil a sense of power, boosting the young man's confidence. He wanted him at his best all the time.

JADEA STARTED ENGINEERING an attack. They discussed it going through each and every step on the paper. A government had started a station that was in the middle of construction to store public and national files. Jadea had heard about this station from other people that wanted to work with him and steal copper wires located in the station.

The operation had about fourteen people, and because it had to be done carefully that gave them enough two weeks to cut them slowly and unnoticed. This operation continued for a number of days that they were cutting some wires loading them in cargo.

> A master does not fall asleep just because his servants have done so, he keeps his eyes open planning for the day after tomorrow. Challenges are meant to be conquered, scored goals are admirable and then if a team does not score any goals, the other team will. Is it good to be religious? Yet, the hearts remaining hard!

They used the drain pipes to carry them all the way to an open area. After a prolonged two weeks, they'd a very big truck ready to transfer the cargo to Mozambique for buyers. The whole truck carried the number of wires worth about fourteen million rand.

The last day they pulled out the cables, the city had a blackout, which left the whole city in a shock and impatient for answers. When the mayor and investigators arrived, the truck was almost close to the border leaving the country.

NEIL WAITED TO SEE the results of the copper robbery. The police also thought everything was coming through as the mayor pressurized them for results. The damage amounted to about five times to what was stolen, the contractors nearly pulled out because of the insufficient funds to move on with the construction.

The mayor kept on talking about what had happened, even the newspapers were bought just to catch his next statements.

The copper drivers delivered the goods accordingly, and then they were packed into containers for shipping to another continent.

When all this was done, Neil pulled out of the brown bag delivery business as Jadea had told him that this was no longer a game for them. In those weeks, Neil was paid in large amounts. When he saw it, amazingly he knew his life had changed.

> People are involved in commercial acts, arts and influence for a small percentage, for example, commercial music, they support a very unhealthy lifestyle, and it is all business. A parent wouldn't like it or support it when children are often drunk and high, it's a waste of life and money. Drunkards, excessive smoking, syrup, and prostitution that have caused many diseases among both young and old people started from this influence and pressure.

Since he took the money and used it as capital to grow his record label. With enough lights and cameras, meeting new people and making his mother proud like never before, this marked a new start. He started changing many things.

If everything that had happened would reach the public ear, probably that was going to jeopardize his business. He thought to stop dealing and robbing for money just to get his dreams to come true, it took him more than a year to have substantial equipment.

When all this was happening, he learned never to trust anyone including his closest friends.

Walking away from Jadea was walking away from money, but at some point, it had to happen. They laid low for some time using the money wisely. The first album was vibrant and sales increased after they shot three videos from that album.

His story of success and making it big was quite the right one, and those who judged from an outside perspective thought of it as greatness.

What they were writing in their lyrics sounded as if it related to personal struggles. A combination of freedom, love and the streets in the same album.

At first, those who took their time listening to it, they would say, "we once heard about it," but that did not matter to Neil.

He kept on pushing creativity increasing his skill and developing patterns to rap on any beat. Those who came to his shows were never disappointed, every time he had a new song for his fans.

> The way that the five percent of the world is making money through ninety-five percent, both educated and uneducated are living to default. It is not wrong to be rich and have wealthy, but it is how one gets rich that makes it evil. Both poor and rich are motivated by faith and hope. However, Poverty does not mean a person's consciousness is very high, poverty has a negative impact and it is widely discouraged.

However, sometimes he was home with his family, usually his son and his baby mother. He took out some books that he had bought pertaining to war and biographies of war heroes. He took his time reading them and understanding purposes of life. He read some spiritual books also.

Neil Hadebe was facing a war within himself more than with anyone else or the world. He saw the happiness around his family, he could provide and he had opened a company already at the age of twenty-three. His conscious mind challenged him to do better before making his decisions. The reputation had prevailed like the south wind, respect grew and a fleet of women chased his fame and champagne bottles.

They were happy about how life was treating them, a flawless dream. Jadea called and asked him to meet at their usual club:

"One thing that I do is to blame myself for my failures so that I can do better next time and every time. I prefer to do overtime even if it is hard most of the time, at least it is the right time usage. We might earn all this money, but we cannot earn time and keep some for our budgets. Life is a journey of trials and tribulations," Jadea believed.

Neil said, "since we are talking about life, I have this new music thing going well and I want to improve in it so much that it can provide for my family and with all due respect, I want to thank you for helping me out since day one, when I did not deserve it, but I think it is time for me to do my own thing."

Jadea placed his hand into the pocket and took out a shining black stone.

"THIS CARBONADO, commonly known as the "black diamond", it is the toughest form of a natural diamond. It is an impure form of polycrystalline consisting of diamond, graphite and amorphous carbon. It is found primarily in alluvial deposits in the Central African Republic and in Brazil.

Its natural colour is black or dark grey, and it is more porous than other diamonds. It is a black diamond born out of flames and violence. A volcanic glass."

"Is it that expensive on the market? Neil asked.

Jadea replied saying, "it depends on what you call expensive, some things are priceless, in about three months we have a job on the way. Then after that, you could go and live your musical life. We have to start planning now so that we can be clean with our way out."

"What is this job about? Neil asked.

"It's a safe box full of black diamonds. And will never have money problems again in life," Jadea replied.

Jadea had one life mission and that was to hit Joey Moore. A man who once dissed him in front of his brothers. When Joey Moore insulted him in front of people it hurt Jadea badly.

He made it a racial issue, which made more sense to him that time, but it had nothing to do with that, a little misunderstanding turned into a mess. That soundlessly added issues on top of other issues Jadea grew up with.

> Whoever is humble serve those under him. A person motivated by revenge is trapped by his own heart of vengeance. Vengeance eats away the core part of a soul, the most powerful revenge is forgiveness because forgiveness mends a broken heart and sets it free. Forgiving an enemy avoids one to be as bad as his enemies. When one does not forgive they are likely to do something that is not worth of mercy.

THEY CONCLUDED the conversation and took separate ways. Whilst Neil was on his way home, Tammy phoned him. She called him for a lift, they had both planned to have dinner at his mother's place. He drove there and picked her up, and because of all the hustles he had in previous days and months. Neil bought a car registered as a company property. Tammy had bought some groceries that they placed at the back seat. They were discussing many different issues between them, they were now used to each other's different opinions.

He shared most of the stories and a few secrets with her. Some of the deep secrets, he kept her in the dark because the trust between them barely existed. In good days they avoided arguing. It was not every time they agreed on the same thing.

Although, at times, they would argue over simple matters. If a relationship is only based on money, the moment there is a shortage of it in that relationship, it breaks into pieces.

It took time for them to settle many issues, but after a period of quarrels, she would be as sweet as ever just to make up for the lost time. Tammy did not give in to mend broken pieces as competition had increased towards her man.

Neil's mother welcomed them with a hot meal as usual. She talked more about life. She then said to them, "You too should come to church this coming Sunday, we have a very large meeting for young married people like you."

Neil, however, replied quickly when his mother intentionally mentioned marriage.

"Ma, we are not married, we just had a baby together and nothing extra to that."

"My son," she said, then she started laughing thinking about her childhood, and that her son was just old enough to make his own decision.

> Some poor people have such a mentality that a rich person owns him\her something, which is totally wrong. A bad attitude is judging a person because of his\her wealthy. God's favorites are those that truly love him and respect him. Stop burdening someone to give out something. We bore that responsibility, as a whole, we should love each other beyond one's knowledge.

A quite remarkable young man wearing professional formal expensive suits six days each week. Everything happens for a reason and it is just a matter of looking at it from a positive perspective because to fail is to see a problem in a matter, instead of answers in every problem. Neil went to his old room and his mother took his son to her bedroom. She convinced them that Junior would remain behind with her for a couple of days.

"I do not see my grandson that much, so at least he should remain behind, I am always alone in this big house," she needed something to do worth a while.

Neil did not disagree with it, because it was going to be a never ending argument between them. She also suggested that the following Sunday, they would first go to church together before collecting him. He agreed and realized that is it the only way he could get family time. Jadea taught him to be constantly family caring because it is the only way to keep them in the dark and out of sight while he hustles for them.

> Wealth is defined in two ways, either rich in spirit or rich financially, and everyone is entitled to have both. Do not expect to receive each and every time, it is a pit that a person envies against others, but expect to give every time as much as you expect to receive. For a wealthy person learn to give out of your good heart like it is an obligation.

Sometimes Neil would be stressed with business when some artists were not putting a hundred percent work in the studio, his concern was both good music and marketing profit. Whenever he was having a meeting with all the people he partnered with, they would do a meeting while having some drinks and good food.

This was an approach to keep minds free and businesses going. In this way, he knew those who were playing him and those who were serious, if he was going to make something real and a legacy for his son and other children to follow, obliviousness was not an option. When people are drinking, smoking, and eating, they usually tell secrets.

Neil being around his mother for advice was as if he was king Lemuel. She then opened the last chapter of the proverbs book in her bible and showed him a couple of verses. She lamented;

> "My son, my son of my womb and vows, do not waste your strength on women, on those who ruin kings. It is not for Kings to guzzle wine. Rulers should not crave alcohol. For if they drink, they may forget the law and not give justice to the oppressed. Alcohol is for the dying, and wine for those in bitter distress. Let them drink to forget their problems and remember their troubles no more. Speak up for those who cannot speak for themselves; ensure justice for those being crushed. Yes, speak up for the poor and helpless, and see that they get Justice."

The nave of the church was now filled with seats for the use of the congregation. They sat in a church service, the Church Leader preached about repenting and living right. As he was talking about it, Neil felt the need to change and his consciousness grew a bit by bit.

He would listen unobtrusively as if the words preached were directly talking about his way of living. He silently questioned where his life was going, he had enough money to leave all the unworthy gambles of life behind.

Never in once was Jadea ever going to let him off the hook. He had a chance to write his own story. He wrote down the verse that the preacher said, "For what shall it profit a man if he shall gain the whole world, and lose his own soul?

They left the church and went home for lunch, like a new man Neil talked about change and choosing love over everything. He then realized that many young people under his company were only focusing on the benefits, they were not finding inner music voices.

He asked his manager to get other recording companies music contract drafts. Ambitions for all things of the world like "money" and "fame" are good, but they are temporary, ways to achieve them requires constant hard work.

The next day, Monday morning he went to all the studios checking which producer was doing better and putting effort, he had invested money in upgrading his studios. Seeing them idle did not go well with him.

His high hopes of music as a career grew as days passed. Learning such things only requires persistent and love in what you do. Skills are developed and expertise are used in serving others equally.

Neil went into his studio and started working on some new beats, usually, he would let others mostly those who were in business with him to handle paperwork, but he recorded all money transactions. They listened to some instrumentals whilst writing rhymes on a notepad including poets. He spent his whole day recording music.

> Everyone should learn to be productive because laziness only lands one into a tunnel of jealous and wishful thinking. Work harder than yesterday and the day before yesterday, and you will never give a burden to others. Have the heart to give every time.

It takes these steps to be a hit-maker, some wants the harvested fruits without effort and work in the first place. Music is just someone's trade and many work as players waiting for a substitute.

During the same afternoon, Jadea called Neil to come over, so that, he would show him plans for their next mission, this was the last hard robbery for them and a perfect life-changing moment. Jadea followed up every story about Joey Moore, he wanted to know where the man lives, his family, his favourite restaurants, his enemies, his cars and his mistresses.

Jadea kept on digging until he found out that this man had been in the industry for a very long time, selling and buying hot or blood diamonds. Joey kept a safe box in his bedroom full of diamonds, this was part of his own treasure gathered for a number of years.

Clearly, Joey over-protected these diamonds with a caution. He killed many and buried some alive with a shovel just to keep those diamonds in his hands only. A ruthless and a savage man is not defined by skin colour, age or sex, but with actions.

> Righteous living is the love of sharing that means everyone has one goal, which is to be one as a whole, one love beyond race deception. Colour is not a restriction and neither is a culture. An honest heart is a way for a better living, remember at some point rich or poor, kind or unkind, king or servant and president or civilians, we all die living this wealthy behind.

However, can someone afford honesty more than once in every business when paying their own employees? People love money so much that it is never enough. It is compared to jealous when it closes one's eyes and leaves them forever blind. We are all disturbed from what can actually happen if we stop focusing on money. We are blinded by what we love most. Some in power remain silent as some products have become the cause of addictions and very unhealthy for people.

Neil became determined to become better while going through all kinds of phases, change started making an impact on his life. Times shadowed, he followed his mother to church to do the Will of God. He was a young man under the influence of the world.

It was time to make a decision that would make his life a testimony or something totally different. He quietly chose to go and work with Jadea on this last job. In the studio, he was finishing his second album which had more work to be done than just thoughts and procrastination.

Life is short as others interpret it. A well-lived lifetime is full of ever young inspirations and memories; it is the immortality of a soul. So, if you feel like your face is not yellow enough to be beautiful then understand, it is not a face that is ugly but a soul. Matter is only mind in an opaque condition; and all beauty is but a symbol of spirit. This is a big meaningless world to educate children about morals, but yet it is still important to teach them that.

For that instant, everything that surrounds us daily in our lives is influenced by what we hear and what we watch. It is the same with alcohol and syrup, it is easy to start all these things but stopping it requires total devotion.

The owners of these products instead of pulling them out of the markets and fix the addiction in them, they usually let these products stay in the market shelves because of profits. Many syrup products that have codeine in them are widely abused. Nevertheless, for the sake of profits the world is dying. Young people are great consumers of commercial products. Many products are destroying the ordinary society as depression is increasing among the teens, and a misinformed society supports these products.

Chapter 06 - Brothers

LIKEWISE, HIS POETRY AND message changed from other musicians' perspective on music and above all his fans, but the problem remained that it was hypocrisy to preach about change while he was struggling with change himself.

He wrote a verse, "Getting hooked with a joint is like ovule egg fertility." He meant smoking at first could be entertaining, but when one gets pleasure, enjoyment, diversion, amusement, or relaxation, addictions kicks in and takes over. Neil Hadebe believed music would be a getaway and a chance for him to change, and his lyrics remained a symbol of his emotions and public image.

> How could it be that everyone wishes to change and do well without devotion? A change of heart only follows after obedience and sacrifices. With words of mouth, many have changed. When everyone is doing it that does not mean it is the right thing to do. Wordlessly, we are born to stand out of the norms.

Implicitly, he saw that an increase in the audience requires personal growth to be able to give audiences something matured. Either to a real game player or a hypocrite, they were just rapping for money and nothing else but fame. He had made money already through Jadea, but rapping for more money was much of a burden, he just wanted to do it for entertainment.

Neil's second album was missing two last songs when Jadea called him for work. Jadea told him that the plan had changed, Neil had to come through that night. The young man left everything and packed his bag for business. Neil heard rumours about Jadea killing his best friend after a betrayal. These rumours scared him the most and he feared to be next.

He packed his satchel and placed his gun on the waist. Jadea sent him the address of the place they'd agreed to meet at the designated time.

> However, change can be delusional if misunderstood as much as false information spreads often because it is interesting, and usually the truth spreads slowly and it is a matter of understanding it. The working class receives annuals and from that everything is perfect. Ambitions born from the pain of poverty keeps the ungrateful nature within a person greedy for more, whilst unaware.

Jadea told him that night, "the place we going is far and a flight is easy and fast, although it will give us hard time because of weapons. I have booked two tickets for a bus that is leaving at ten o'clock at night. I hope you have carried everything you want because we are not coming back after a couple of days."

They went to a rank and boarded a bus that was going to take them to another close city for a hunt. They talked about life and how miserable the churches had become with many hypocrites hiding the truth and people accepting lies, and exchanging the truth with nuts, and as usual, they didn't discuss about the actual truth and those that are actually doing it correctly.

That night they travelled a very long distance. They reached the region that Joey and his wife Lisa were living in. It was around three in the morning when they arrived. Jadea had already set-up a car to use. They took it from someone he had made a deal with on the phone. They drove into a suburb while wearing black, from top to bottom.

When they were in that suburb they drove slowly and the area was well guarded with some community securities. Jadea dropped off before they had arrived at the main gate.

> There is poverty on earth as food is never enough when water is a shortage. Equivalent to excess of resource should not be based on the flag of colors, because under the earth we are all a family. When destruction comes, it does not choose a country, area or religion of people, it will destroy everything.

Jadea wanted to find a way to enter inside, and especially during that time, everyone is very cautious about whose knocking at their gate. He knew the house like the owners. It took him time while studying it, in and out. When he dropped off, he used one of the neighbour's houses to jump into Mr. Morish's yard also known as Mr Moore. They noticed that the security guard was sleeping.

It's not every time that we expect someone to knock at 03H00 in the morning, they confidently caught him off guard. When he went into the yard the security officer heard nothing. Jadea had direct access to silence this man temporarily. He slowly pointed his gun at him. The officer heard the footsteps and woke up with speedy and trauma, although he remained quiet.

Jadea forced him to open the gate at gunpoint. Neil drove the car inside. The people that were sleeping in the house were not aware of all these activities in a very big yard.

Jadea asked the Officer at the gate the number of people that were in the house, and how to get rid of all the alarms. When this happened, it was like taking a candy from a baby. After getting rid of alarms, they tempted with the electricity main board. The main house's electricity went off. They left the security officer tied to a chair in a dark corner.

Jadea walked to the main bedroom with two pistols in his hand. He kicked the door and it open at once. That second, an electric system separated from the ordinary home appliances went on to replace the one they'd tempted with.

All the sudden, the bang on the door woke Joey up in fear. Joey tried to reach for his gun to protect his wife as she was in terror. His pistol was in the safe-box, which he could not reach instantly. He wanted to say something to calm the situation down. Fears of losing his wife stroke him.

Rich countries have a tendency to remain all-powerful and majestic through the natural resources of other poor countries.

In each civilization, there is a repetition of style in all ages to the eras of Egypt and before it. Several dominions have followed the maniac adopted ideas of conquering the whole world. Such an idiotic thinking has been followed for ages and studied through all the centuries.

"How can I help fellows? Joey took his trousers laid next to his bed.

Jadea removed his black mask and asked, "do you remember me, brother?

Joey left his bed and walked away from it and said, "What do you want here? You have overstepped and this is too far." Neil did not remove his mask like Jadea.

Jadea replied, "This is simple, what is behind that wall picture?

He pointed with his pistol to a wall frame. Joey Moore knew exactly what Jadea was talking about. He walked closer to the wall next to the bed and took down the picture. Jadea stood aware that something might be hidden in the safe besides diamonds, a weapon rather.

It remains the same reason why a poor man, Jesus Christ was crucified when he preached life giving gospel and healed the poor of this world, it is not a philosophy, regardless of colour, and the nature of an individual, which many people until today have refused to recognize and understood.

He walked nearer, but not too very close because Joey was a well-trained tactical man.

Neil Hadebe on the other bedside had his gun pointed at Lisa. They thought this would keep Joey steady, constant and focused. Unfortunately, Joey had a very different mentality.

If anything was ever going to happen, it was taking down two amateurs in his bedroom. In just a moment, when he opened the safe, Jadea warned him to stay away from it.

Somehow in a flash, Joey's impatient nature cost him his life.

Neil only said to Lisa, "Don't do anything stupid." Joey reached out for the gun in that safe quickly. Jadea fired a shot at him. While falling down, Joey's finger pressed the trigger and shot Jadea on the neck.

These two people blasted each other to death with single shots. Neil ran and collected the guns off the floor. Lisa jumped off the bed with her eyes pouring tears all over her dead husband's body lying down next to their bed. Thinking otherwise, Neil collected the guns and everything that was in the safe box.

Lisa remained quiet looking at her husband on the floor. Neil took a sheet on the bed and covered Jadea's body that he carried out to the car. He placed the corpse in the boot wrapped in a bed sheet. What happened was unexpected and the community security had not been alarmed yet.

Jadea's heart could not forgive Joey. The issue between them was more than robbing diamonds, it was personal.

Neil drove the car to the nearest forest located close to that suburb. He dug a grave in that forest for about three hours.

> Today, we have many systems invested in the world of the matrix that deceives and victimizes masses of people. Such gigantic ideas fed into the minds of many are converted into a living dream. Once upon a time, children used to lose innocence at eighteen, but nowadays, we have an increase in the level of child pornography and child sex cases.

The whiskey bottle they had reserved for celebration was almost half empty. He poured some onto Jadea's graveyard. He took his lighter and poured whiskey into the car. He threw the lighter into the car. Neil did not stick around to watch it happen, so he left a burning car on top of this ditch. He washed his hands on a close-by pond.

Afterward, he went to a mall looking for a GYM company. It was possible that they'd showers inside. This was the same city that the police had started searching for him, the car and Jadea's corpse.

In one of the shops, they were selling very expensive clothes. He took out some money avoiding using his card which was the only second thing in his pocket. He bought a formal black suit.

WHEN HE FOUND A SHOWER at the GYM, he paid for a monthly service in order to just using it once. Subsequently, he was clean and ready for his trip back home for new business. Everything for him as a twenty-three-year-old had changed compared to the lives of those of his age.

He went to a bus station searching for a bus to board back home. His bag was next to him. All this time everything seemed satisfactory, although he was paranoid so much to settle his mind at one place.

His thoughts kept on replaying the images of Joey and Jadea killing each other.

The new guilt conscience started entertaining his thoughts. Two men had died and he had played a part in it for diamonds. These were results of hatred.

Jadea, when he was young during the days of segregation. His brother and mother were shot in front of him and that left his father a drunkard.

From that, he learned nothing but hatred for the Caucasian man and that part of him never healed. Joey made a mistake the day he ill-treated this man. It only caused him to remember his mother and brother's unhealed wounds.

Few are maturing inside because their focus is outside appearance. We are moving into a future that focuses on the outside beauty as much as it is advertised in every corner. Real advantages of growth are inside of us; our souls are worth more than gold. Love grows inside and it is experienced outside. A person who has problems with drugs cares less about his outside appearance as much as he cares for his intimate being. He wants to be high inside not outside.

A drunkard father could not do anything to cover the wounds Jadea had. His father lost a wife and a son that day. He blamed himself as a man that he could not protect them. And he sort comfort in drinking thinking that it would ease up the pain but that made it worsened everything.

While he was oblivious, his remaining son grew up to hate Caucasian people. Jadea robbed houses after dropping out of school. His cousin brother Foster picked him up in the mud after he had been arrested for breaking an entry.

They found dirty jobs together with very high profile customers. Jadea matured from that point onwards, but his temper remained a problem that he could not overcome. He did business with an iron rod. He created many enemies and that made him live by a gun from time to time.

NEIL REGARDED HIMSELF AS rich. He thought money was happiness, but he still felt empty and sad. He tried to write a song and something poetic to change his mood and twisted emotions.

He felt like Joey's death was his fault and Jadea would be alive, if he didn't just stand idle. Such a feeling and desperation drove him crazy.

> Whoever or whatever that affects inside is dangerous or very important above all. An outside expression is only set to make one forgets about focusing on the intimate nature as it rots away. One day the world is going to fall with everything in it, and can one live without all these things that surround us especially in developed countries, our wealthy.

His son crossed his mind and getting arrested once again was bad for his new reputation and image. He couldn't just imagine the thoughts of his mother crying because of him.

He arrived home at around 16H00. He took what was in the bag and placed it on top of the wardrobe. He left the house to a close-by church. When he arrived in the church there was another service already taking place. He joined in and sat on one of the chairs. The Pastor was preaching and discussing the life of King Solomon.

The Pastor preached, "With all the wealth and wisdom the world had ever known, Solomon still could not find happiness. One woman after another, whatsoever the world defined it as happiness, whilst it was a struggle for Solomon. Do not search for happiness in material things, but in the Lord Christ Only."

"Happiness that is brought by material things is temporary and it is always unsatisfactory." He left the church after the Pastor closed the service with a prayer.

What eyes sees affects the whole soul, then why do we all live to satisfy the eyes that cannot take a glance on the inside nature of a person? Change is not religious or tribal. It is personal and surprisingly, we have been groomed into a whole bunch of material lovers forgetting one day everyone dies from the richest to the poorest.

As usual, he criticized the message because that part of happiness could not make him smile more than he wanted too.

Making money was always the dream, and when it happened to him, he had the chance to be on top of the world. The love of money tormented his thoughts, his hands were dirtier than before.

He bought some marijuana after the church service. He drove his car and went to his place of business like nothing had happened. When he heard about the release of his correctional facility friend, he stopped focusing on his problems and became concerned about his friend's arrival.

His closest friend Mhazi Chuma had just been released from a correctional facility. Mhazi decided to join them to make music together. All his burning ambitions to make music and do something positive in his life kept him in the studio countless times waiting for Neil.

After smoking excessively, it was time for music. With confidence, these young people had different dubious and miscellaneous characters.

Their love for hip hop and music, in general, was worth sacrificing everything. Neil sensed that compromising quality for money was unnecessary. It has become a priority for many musicians both young and old to compromise quality music for quantity.

He just wanted to be different from other musicians. If that was the case, then he had to be honest with himself first. Young minds are full of dreams that expect successes overnight. Dreams that are bigger requires bigger sacrifices, it might be time, money, friends or relationships, but in the end, it is all worth it. Neil's conscience constantly reminded him about his deeds.

"On ne fait pas d'omelette sans casser les oeufs." One cannot make an omelette without breaking the eggs first, and then whatever people do, it has consequences either today or tomorrow.
Humble is such a great word that is followed by a few deeds. Pride and humbleness mostly live in two separated rooms. Moderately, only a few are humble in life, poor or rich it matters not.

He spent the following weeks attending Church services to fill in his spiritual emptiness. He tried alcohol, but it was not getting him anyway. He added syrup on his bucket list to get more drunk, but that seemed to be just an ordinary cough mixture adding loneliness.

Others snorted cocaine to get high, but Neil avoided it even though he could afford it. He lost the urge for sex for a while, this type of depression was unusual. He knew that only the truth would set him free. The question was, "why the guilt like I did something wrong?

During the same weeks that he was attending these services, it seemed like a joke when he tried the Lord's Prayer. He could not remember the words.

That simply showed him the lifestyle he wanted most and liked so well was never good for him. He was counselled by one of the youths in the church. The desperations increased with pain and burden. On the other hand, his mother's prayers strengthened him. She was proud of looking at her son growing up into a good man.

Others are lost in trying and in doing road shows entertaining many eyes. Each person judges the next one according to money and glory, mistakes and language, colour and dressing, and this fall under one particular category and this category allows pride and proud to live happily unsatisfied.

A person who preaches to others about winning should be a winner. A person who preaches "let's love each other" that person should love others. Furthermore, whatever positivity that one person promotes, that person should be positive enough to stick to these words.

Whenever a person is giving hope to others, that same person has to respect and obey the words of hope that his mouth is speaking of. Should anything bad happens to that person, the same hope that he once preached to others must remain in him during his trials and tribulations. Nonetheless, we live in a world that is full of rude and stubborn people.

When such a mass crowd is given a bit of wise advice many of them run into conclusion looking for a mistake in every sentence to the point that they forget all the good words and only remember the bad ones. The truth hurts masses and helps few. Having wisdom is totally different from being smart. A smart child performs well in all the assignments but fails to learn simple ways of life among others. A modern child adapts the way of living like others, but a wise child observes both a smart child and modern child's mistakes, whatever is good between them, he\she applies and anything bad or wrong that comes from these two he\she throws it away with rubbish.

Making a better living and being totally able to afford something is not always based on the level of education a person has. But surely it could be based on the amount of wisdom a person has. The wisdom from God is ever young. It allows an individual to adapt to any and every situation. It is the same wisdom that Solomon the King had, yet during his era wisdom was scarce. Humbleness is part of wisdom. This is the first step of understanding. Whenever a problem arises, most people have a tendency to complain or actually dig deeper into the problem creating more problems expecting someone else to fix them.

Chapter 07 - Don't forget the forgotten

Christina was stuck with her investigation, but the death of Joey came to her attention as a new baby born. As it was, she attended to her duties in the most perfunctory and superficial manner. Her concerns about Joey's death were somehow great. And his death was unexpected. His death drew more ears and eyes to the story. He was a well-respected member of his society and a former member of the army.

> The only solution to every problem starts from the core of a changed mindset, a problem changes into a challenge and challenges could be conquered. Stealing never keeps wealthy in one's hands, in either way, it destroys or kills. Many people in this world find it easier to get rich through the pain of others. No matter how big life can be at some point, if a business only tempers with the truth and treat justice as a joke, doubtlessly, mental breakdowns are experienced due to stress. A good example is Bernard Madoff whose whole family suffered most because of a lie.

IT WAS ONLY A MATTER of time before one of the former government officers had fallen from power. She again gave a call to Marvin to come over and help her reopen the closed case that they'd already gave up on.

The only witnesses with answers were Joey's wife Lisa and the security guard. When homicide investigators arrived for interrogation, Lisa was mourning and in pain. She told them exactly what had happened the morning her husband died.

For the fact that Joey died in his house and the dead murderer's sketch that came from the description Lisa gave the police that morning traced back to one of the people Joey had previous worked with, and coincidences in homicide case do not exist.

This raised a question of a possible conspiracy. Why did they turn against each other? This was the question detectives had in mind. They sniffed like dogs taking on an unresolved case. They were determined to go to Joey's house, and even to ask exactly what happened the day the man was shot and how it got to that point.

> Life has many medals and none of them last forever. Even if we educate each and every human being to put them in use, whose education last always? Human beings are living in an era where technology and other advancement have increased rapidly in a very short space of time, and the end of it is missiles.

Joey never kept a camera in his bedroom. Lisa stopped him for private reasons. The other cameras did not capture much after the whole system was shut down during the robbery.

Lisa explained how that situation left her devastated. This case was not covering exactly what had been robbed in the house. How did it get to be that the robbers killed such a gun expert? They'd experienced many endeavours throughout homicides, but this was a tough one to ever occur in the force. Each and every one of the victims was a well-known Officer.

Sergeant Joey had worked for the army for some time, and his work was clear enough to be considered a person who had served the country honourably. He survived through loopholes and looting.

Neil felt guilt for what he had done. Either he thought, to live with it or to die broke and imprisoned. He almost gave up, but this was just the beginning of a whole bigger world for him.

His mother cooked dinner, as usual, a mother saw the worries of her child from a distance. She had to ask when the dinner was almost over.

> Communications and languages have become familiar and easy, which at one point might be an act of union among all nations and flags. When communication and language develop easily such as nowadays, the end results are disastrous and irreversible.

"What is it that you are thinking about the child of my womb? I can see that something seems to have your attention, what is it?

Neil asked her, "Mama, how often do people get second chances in life? How often is a person forgiven and do people literally change into completely new individuals?

She answered him, "Yes, my son, people do change, but never just by themselves, why do you think Jesus Christ was crucified in the first place? It is because people can change, that is what he taught us. Only by knowing him you can be changed forever and never again to do your bad and old habits. It is your choice my womb."

They finished up their dinner, the conversation changed. Afterward, Neil helped his mother to pack up dishes.

He said, "I was hoping for a sleepover, then again I still have some busy work to do. We are launching an album for one of our new artists and I have to be there for the launch." She hugged him and he left.

> Many people are now going into what is called a 'sleeping mode', living in a world without scars. If the minds of people were to unite to build each other spiritually and increasing intellectual reasoning, all the first world countries would not be spending time building missiles against each other.

Surely, the diamonds from Joey's safe-box were certainly priceless and he was going to sell them. They were still illegal diamonds worth millions.

The police looked for the vehicle that Neil used for days. After looking around in the area tracing road cameras one after another, the street surveillance traced the car, but they couldn't find it until someone found it and reported it.

They dragged the car away as part of evidence and found Jadea's body on. They took the Deoxyribonucleic acid (DNA) test. The body had decayed and Neil did not dig deep enough, the smell of a dead body was all over the place. They collected the evidence.

The homicide crew surrounded the whole area and started looking for further lines of trace. Whatever Lisa had told them about the morning her husband got shot, it probably made more sense when the investigation corresponded with her answers.

THEY EXAMINED THE BODY thoroughly and it matched with blood samples retrieved from the house. Finding out the man who shot Joey was easy. The other individual was still out there somewhere spending the money or whatever they had robbed in the house. Lisa did not specify exactly what was stolen.

Everything was going to turn sour if the investigators were to understand that these were diamonds illegally smuggled. Instead of them being used by the state, other individuals used them for personal securities. She lied to protect her husband's honour. She knew about these diamonds and it was better if the police had stopped investigating them. She had to protect herself from this. The police kept on telling her, "we will help you to honour your husband."

In our human civilizations, we have always been preparing for wars, sharpening knives to kill each other for glory.

What is the improvement during the courses of time? If the same wars and the same mentality of domination remains amongst us! When we think about glory, none of the people living on the planet deserves any. It is not a matter of believing to understand but the greater power is there and above all.

It was during that period when Christina came through just to see who was in charge of this investigation. She did not interfere, Christina being around these investigations raised questions to the Officers that were in charge.

"Hello, Ms." one of the Officers walked close to Christina.

"How can we help you? This is a private investigation and by any means can you please excuse this crime scene, if you are not of any help."

Christina produced her police identity card. The police officer who was talking to her walked away. They were both investigators. Christina's face remained unfamiliar to all these Policemen.

Furthermore, the death of Joey left his enemies upset and happy at the same time. One man, in particular, it was just a few days after the man's death when George received a call from one of his friends in the police force.

"JOEY IS NOW DEAD after being smoked out by some robbers at his own residents." George wanted to get excited when he heard this on the phone. They hated each other, only wishing death for one another, but the reality remained petrifying.

George kept it to himself for a while. 'Who had the guts to kill this man? The caller sounded as if everything went well with the robbers.

George wondered who these killers were. His long term rival had just died. He wished this man's death for a very long time. The cause of death remained unbelievable to his ears and eyes, yet expected at some point. He paid close attention to daily news.

The story became clearer each time the reporters spoke about it. All George wanted to know was the man behind the majestic plan that killed Joey Moore. Police did not reveal that for privacy reasons.

DESPITE THE FACT THAT others were busy using their nails scrubbing the ground to find lost treasure. Neil was burning with everlasting lust. When weeks of stress had passed and the pressure was gone. Everything went back to normal. They went to one of the top city clubs.

> Due to our own reasoning capacity and the type of education we acquire in the days of our lives, we are forced into living and believing only what eyes can see. Then, who is better in this case, the one without eyes at all or the one who lives only because of his eyes.

The waiter brought them some hookers, ice, and whiskey. Beyond a shadow of doubt, they could afford all this. All he wanted from that night was having two to three women to sleep with. This life of a rap star is nothing without a guard. It was time to start focusing on the fruits of his labour.

His urge for sex that night was something that he could not measure. He ignored that he had a girlfriend home, almost a wife. Then again, he refused to acknowledge that title to her. He would always say, "we only had a child together." He still had not forgiven her for not visiting him in prison.

Neil took it personally and told her at some point of their argument that she was only around because he wanted someone to look after the baby with proper care. No other woman was ever going to be a better mother than the mother herself. However, having her around so much, at first was annoying but love grows.

They ordered some whiskey in the club. While he was in the club, many girls noticed them and that drew attention, they thought "these people are rich," as they were drinking expensive alcohol.

> Judgmental are the same eyes, lustful are the same eyes and hopeless are the eyes. True change is within a heart, and a mind that has been changed only seeks more transformation and to show others the Way. The first world countries have come to a point of deciding whom to ban or which country to ban from this trade or that trade.

Mostly, the girls that approached them were students between the age of eighteen and twenty-five. Neil and his crew brought cars, it was easy to leave with these girls after the party. Surprisingly, the young females were so excited that these hot-boys were taking the party back to a five-star hotel.

Beautiful clueless women in the club dancing half-naked and pulling low-lives men into their lives.

They enjoyed the whole night. In the morning when he arrived home, the first question his baby mother asked, "Where have you been? I waited the whole night hoping you will show up from work, but when I called your phone it was off and they said you knocked off at work yesterday at 13H00. So, I ask again, where were you last night? Neil looked at her and walked to his bed.

"Unbelievable," he thought. She felt stupid, that he did not fight back and engage in a quarrel with her. He felt exhausted after the night.

Neil had something to work for and to live for, and if the shoe fits wear it. They could afford anything so they calculated their own budget for a new music video that could be played national wide. They worked on the song first and possibly with good ears on it.

Only wicked people agree with a country banning another country from trading, yet, the banners swim in honey and milk, while the children in countries banned from trading serve as an example of poverty and dreadful disease.

Organizations sit to have a meeting of destruction just to punish one person in a country with millions of starving individuals, the conversation goes like this, "we control the food, and then, we control people."

It turned out that their sound engineers were focused. After a great turn of events, they hosted music video shoots which took them more than four weeks, to hire cars, renting buildings and woman to dance in the video half-naked.

They made researches about music video marketing style and shooting style, and the targeted audience. They listened to one of the marketers and video production expert elaborating about mistakes made during shootings, and advertising products that have nothing to do with video promotion. Neil had done three videos from his previous album, but they were not as successful as expected.

They were organized. They made sure that this fourth music video had no mistakes. It had to be bombarding. They directed the video properly. It was edited by another production company, and it took two weeks before their video had started playing in one of the most famous music channels in the country regularly.

Someone had informed them to pay money for bribery to the television producers to be played constantly. They were ready to play the same game that everyone was playing. Not everything was about music.

> This will go on as the world of Capitalist mentality grows and starving nations are increasing. Sanctions have been imposed on many countries and those same people that have imposed sanctions they have a history of oppression against others.
> We tend to fear for our lives and how hard they might become, but all this prevents us as people to stand up and fight against oppression.

As the case's investigation proceeded, the police department started face recognition along with the pictures that had Jadea in it. They downloaded many contemporary images that featured Jadea with high hopes to apprehend the other culprit.

When George heard Jadea killed Joey, it was unsurprising. He only regretted inspiring Jadea into committing the murder. He quickly phoned Foster to alert him about Jadea's sudden death.

"What a turn of events that happened a few weeks ago," George said. Foster replied muddled unaware of the caller's name and details, "What are you talking about."

"Your cousin is dead and by this, I assume you know nothing." Foster recognized the voice of the caller after paying attention to the call.

"Are you saying Jadea is dead?

When did this happen? Foster asked fiercely.

George calmly said, "It was Joey and they are both dead now, it was a crossfire."

After Foster spoke to George, he picked up a phone and tried calling his cousin, hoping he would pick up. The number went straight to voicemail. Tears started crawling down his chin. Foster scarcely watched the news or read daily newspapers, he would have heard or read about Joey's death news. He packed his bag to visit the city Jadea had lived for years.

When one stands, he\she must be so confident that others will follow to unite. If none of these things happen, then it passes from generation to another generation of captivity. You might have everything in this world but does everyone have those things. Nevertheless, making profits is a never-ending game.

The police gathered all the information they could. They'd already found the first perpetrator. This case was to be closed only after the arrest of the second culprit. The Investigators looked on the internet with every social media account from Facebook to Instagram looking for pictures involving Jadea's friends.

Astonishingly, they found many pictures and collected only three months old pictures. Neil was in those pictures. They searched the names of individuals in the pictures, specifically going through criminal records on each individual's previous activities.

They carefully observed the current life that Neil Hadebe was living. It appeared as an inspiring story from a jailbird to a successful music mogul. This did not stop them from looking into his actions closely.

Investigators followed up on the other two suspects, one of them was just another young man living at the same building that Jadea was living before the incident. It was an expensive place to live especially for those without six figures in their bank accounts.

Another second suspect who had the same height as Neil was just another boy living in the city doing photographing for huge functions. Jadea and this young man had met at an event hosted by one of the biggest celebrities in the country. Mark who was light in complexion had met Jadea at a glamorous event. It was the very same event that Mark (the photographer) and Neil (the rapper) met through Jadea.

The police asked these two young people their whereabouts the morning of the robbery. The photographer remained a suspect when his answers were fragile, although he held no criminal record.

They suspected a lot after asking him, "Did you have any other businesses with Jadea? He panicked a couple of times during questioning. The investigators appeared like they sought to falsely accuse him in order to close the investigation.

During interrogations, Neil sought a meeting with two leading investigation detectives for answers. It was a Tuesday morning when Officers knocked on his door. Tammy opened the gate after the intercom rang. Neil was still in bed around 08H00 when two detectives arrived to meet him.

> When a person transforms totally, he barely repeats old mistakes. In a very negative way, when a person changes, he will be like a child who has started doing drugs or smoking cigarettes. At first, this child plays hide and seek as they are smoking. Nobody notices these things although a family member does recognise a shady behaviour. This keeps on going, effects will reach a time that even parents get tired of it.

DETECTIVES VS NEIL HADEBE

Detective Anotida, "How are you, young man?

He answered, "I am good, how can I help you this morning gentleman, I do not usually get visits these early mornings unless there is something of an emergency."

One of the police Officers replied, "May we come in, we discussed on the phone about the meeting. We are from the police department; we need to ask you questions for an ongoing investigation."

Neil said, "feel free, please come in." Two men walked in ogling around.

Neil, "can I make some tea."

"No, no, we good," they replied.

Neil made one cup of tea and talked to these officers. They sat down on couches.

"Do you know Jadea? They asked.

"Yeah, I know him, he sponsors our company from time to time. He is very supportive of our work," he replied.

"We regret to inform you that he died a few weeks back, but however we are interested about your whereabouts on the morning of 17th march?

He replied with a deep tone, "Perhaps, I cannot remember well to specifically point out the place. I would be lying if I do so, sometimes we get boozed out. What a terrible thing, by the way, what actually happened to Mr. Jadea?

"We found him buried on an offsite. You lost a sponsor that is unfortunate. Since you know nothing about this, we will find our way out and if anything pops out, we will come around again maybe in a bad mood," they replied Neil stood up with them and walked along with them.

Neil exploded with anger, "if I come across anything that might add up to your investigation, I will surely help through although this does not look good on us right now. That man was our role model and now this."

At some point, they start becoming weak as parents to the ears of their own child. Addiction and stubbornness are found within than child. The child is no-long hiding to smoke or do anything. Every day the child denies that it is an addiction.

He left them outside and remained quiet the whole day. He was frustrated to act normal then again something was totally different about the day. Still, that morning when he went back into his bedroom, Tammy asked, "Early morning visits, are those your colleagues? He replied, "Yeah, do not mind them."

Neil knew he was a suspect in the case. He had to find a way out of it. He believed as experienced as these men were, he could find his way out by paying them only. It was going to take time for them to realize the stupidity he made them went through.

A person is innocent until proven guilty. It was a game that he was willing to play all day and all night. That morning Neil had a meeting scheduled up, so he took his bath just like other ordinary days, perfecting all his daily morning routines without failure.

> When a person faces the conversion of a heart and mind positively, it is maybe during the period that one survives a grave danger incident or accident, one such case in that of a person who discovers that they have cancer, or they are sent to prison while innocent or guilty either way.

After weeks and days had passed since Jadea's death this was the first time his conscious could see Jadea screaming for help. "It's just in my mind," he thought.

When George spoke to Foster, he decided from then to stay out of the picture. Foster arrived at Jadea's place overwhelmed by grievance, hoping it was not true his cousin was still alive. For previous months or so, even up to a year, they had bad blood. Only if the claims were true, Foster had to bury his cousin with full ceremonial respect. It wasn't well with him living Jadea to be buried like a prison thug.

> These people face a new discovery of a human being that they did not know before. Such a transformation opens doors for spiritual

understanding. For example, when a person is diagnosed with cancer, they are hopeless at times. They are in a corner forced to give up, overwhelmed by emotions. It is the same time that others split emotions and reasoning into two different worlds. When it happens, a person is transformed and fear converts into strength.

Chapter 08 - Dreamers

KUSH THERAPY MUSIC GROUP (KTMG), this was the group that Neil had founded. The company had started making some positive proceeds. They spent time looking for new beats and new opportunities. However, Neil spends the whole day meeting up with new agents to push them forward and getting ready for the video launch.

> WHAT IS IT THAT MATTERS most in this life? Everything that is being done, or all things that people are living for, it is all in the history books. For years after years, generation after generation, same one goal, and same one dream. People have lived through the same wars and struggles battling their way out of slavery.

He used more money into this as he could. He paid others to pave the way and success in the music industry. They were too concerned with success even if it meant losing their souls in the process. They presumed to be different from other rappers, but it turned out the game is the same, and only different players.

The police talked to Neil and felt he had nothing to hide from them.

Although they knew he was involved, they were not the ones calling shots. He was a role model to other young ones including their own children.

Neil kept going with a matured remorse conscience. Hardcore

drugs and whiskey separated his mind from all these sorts of trouble. One of his producers made his music out of these emotional lines. The group made more music and this increased their skills on the microphone.

Tapping into their music sounded as if they had been in the industry for years. However, most of the time producers were on drugs, after assuming drugs gave them positive energy and an increase in production. What is the purpose of good production? When health is not a priority.

> After freedom from there oppressors, those who claimed freedom for all during slavery picked up their shoes and sandals and fired bullets at each other. Instead of building those things they wanted for everyone. Mostly young people with money spend it on fashion. The mistake is that some soon forgets that fashion is a culture.

Everything seemed to be moving faster than usual. Neil left the diamonds hidden away. Days after the robbery he took a screwdriver and opened an electrical stove. He shoved a wrapped black plastic with diamonds inside the back of the stove. After the police came to his house, he thought of living the country, but change remained invertible.

The homicide squad had Neil's pictures along with other suspects. They were three suspects in all. They went to the deceased house and sat down with the wife. They took out all the pictures of those suspected, assuredly, all suspects had an errand for Jadea. They placed all these pictures on the table.

It seemed ridiculous when Christina mentioned Neil as a prime suspect, but money remained an important factor between Neil and Prison. She told these officers before questioning Lisa to look into Neil's details constantly and thoroughly. She believes a snake doesn't change, only the skin does. A criminal mindset is a lizard tail. These photographs were placed in front of Lisa. She was desperate for answers. The Officers suggested looking closely at Neil than others. Lisa's attention was drawn to the photographer.

It has been celebrated for ages and nothing is new in the fashion world. Life of a celebrity is nothing like how it is painted. Others later regret wasting money following trends instead of spending it on future investments. It all happens in the blink of an eye because we are condemned to music and entertainment.

She then said, "That is him over there and I remember well now." She was just distracted to examine properly. And the two officers had influenced her into choosing the photographer.

"Are you sure it's him? Since you mentioned he had a mask on," the Detective questioned.

She exclaimed, "I would not have pointed at him if I wasn't sure at all. That is him over there and I recognized the shape of his body." As obvious as it was, they could not see that Neil had a criminal record of theft and breaking an entry. For the worst, this case involved murder and the homicide squad treated the circumstances differently based on their experience.

If they'd dug deeper about Neil's bail, the case would have been closed even before going after other suspects. Commonly from a theory point, the young photographer panicked during questioning. The two Officers looked at his job and were not amazed if he was actually a photographer, they wanted to be convinced differently by someone else.

Although, when they were leaving Lisa's house, she gave them some money and they accepted it. This money was in a brown envelope.

One of the Officers suggested it was bad for business and his partner replied to him. "You have started again, doubting like Thomas. If you think your thoughts are right, then we can go back and you will give all this money back to her. This job is easy. All I need right now is for you to play your part."

These were two corrupt policemen investigating a homicide. George paid them to leak information to him.

Detective Anotida said at last, "let's do this, we are dealing with amateurs and non-experienced little folks, it will not be that hard. Instead of arresting this young man Joey's wife claimed as a suspect, they thought it would be better to just plant evidence, and then kill him during the process.

> The hatred grows and power becomes a denominator of every decision. If a struggle is misunderstood, then the legacy is almost close to nothing. In Africa, people are facing financial problems due to misgovernance and limitation of trading because of sanctions placed on the leaders by the world's governing board.

They went into their car and started planning how to kill him. They delayed until mid-night to move in where the photographer about twenty-two years old was living. Photographing was his profession and a passion. He improved his experience in the industry through weddings and other events.

He observed how people just like him were involved in uploading pictures online just for the love of it. He converted it into a business opportunity. He decided to take part in the modern world living.

Officer Anotida and his partner spent the whole day developing an exact silent approach to kill the young photographer. Whilst they were doing all this, it was not the first time they had received money to solve a problem.

On the other hand, Mhazi was busy compiling up his own album. This was his chance to talk about his life to the masses hoping it will put him from one stage to another. He had lived his life as nothing but trouble. Most other recording rappers he was working with would show up late and drunk for a studio session. Occasionally, not prepared or they would not show up at all.

Bogusly, they talked about hustling making millions and becoming biggest music moguls ever lived. Frequently, Mhazi would wait for them in the studio while writing his next songs. He preferred to even spend extra hours and almost sleepless nights working towards his new album which had fourteen tracks.

Friday nights others would go and drink in clubs, but he remained behind working in the studios. He did not have a proper home to live in, so he made music studios his new home.

> All these things are causing more problems such as an increase in crime, unwanted pregnancies, abortions, poverty, and other social problems. Things are changing, and people are changing also. HUMANS, IN GENERAL, are resistant in changing their minds, even in the face of solid evidence. It is this change that people fear most because when it happens, lives are changed.

Officer Anotida and his partner began before midnight to strike like nightmares crawling in the dreams of a child. When they arrived at the flat that the young photographer was living, it was not as fancy as the building that a person who stole money and diamonds would live in. It was clear enough to see the efforts of a young man trying to make a living.

They arrived at the building and received the information from building officers about the room that they were about to visit.

Nonetheless, this shocked the Security Officers, when they tried to figure out why this room had just received two visits at the same time. All visits were police. Two detectives did not notice that Christina was following their moves, and they were one step away from catching up with her.

She took the boy away. She understood that this had nothing to do with justice. It was a money motivated game. When they were in the lift, Christina was in the middle of explaining to the young man something that seemed like a lie.

She said to him, "they are coming for you and I will explain later, but for now, let us just leave and I will tell you everything." The young man grabbed his camera, jacket, and a backpack. He was worried about his life, and about the people that wanted him dead.

Each mind can change, but it is nearly impossible for this to easily happen. When minds have already been convinced that everything is based on a procedure. When an old and unredeemable mind is introduced to something new, even before attempting it, and already in-denial. It is hard to convert a mind that seeks no room for improvement; it is also difficult to change a heart.

Instead of using a lift Christina was thoughtful enough to use the stairs while the young photographer was behind her. He followed her downstairs in a very elated and "partified" state of mind. Two detectives went to knock on the door and waited for someone to open the door for them. They kept knocking.

Without any answer, they quickly banged the door open with a one-foot blow. The Officers shouted "HELLO!"

The water kettle was still on, yet nobody was around. "Stay here! I will check him elsewhere," the detective said.

Detective Anotida ran downstairs checking up every corner and floor. This was not just any type of a coincidence happening in the middle of the night. The detective had a paranoia at that moment.

He reached out to the security officer on the building entrance.

He asked him if he had seen the boy. The Security officer replied, "Of course, I saw the young man just now. He left with another young white woman in her early thirties. Anotida had already suspected Christina was up to something, but he never thought she was smart enough to take over. He took out his phone and called his partner to meet him downstairs.

His partner arrived with energy wondering if Anotida had spotted the boy. And Mark from a distance had his camera in hand taking photos of these detectives leaving the building.

> In every story and life, revenge is a baby born out of jealousy, hatred or mostly pain. Revenge grows like a child from a month old to seventy years old man or woman with too much ego to forgive. In order to satisfy revenge, it will take both the life of a victim and that of a perpetrator. It takes two graves to satisfy revenge.

The two detectives couldn't see Christina and Mark in the dark. They went back to their cars.

"We have another problem in our hands, Christina? We have to check her background properly. We might be walking towards a pitfall unaware."

His partner replied, "What do you suggest we should do? Because we cannot kill her, she is also an Officer and that comes with great risk."

Anotida responded with a vacuous stare which usually rested on his face, and he spoke in a slow, aggravating drawl, "Most likely, I think she knows nothing. Do not panic, we still have the story on our side. She is only stopping us from making further investigations." They drove the car and left in pursuit.

The young photographer was furious and full of questions. He asked Christina many questions. However, Christina was still arguing with the idea of Mark going back to his apartment. The place was no longer safe.

"What do these men want from me? What have I done so wrong?

Is it all about Jadea? He asked questions non-stop.

"What is your actual full name? She asked.

"Mark Mathebe" he answered.

"Okay Mark, breathe in and out. Now listen to me, I know that you are scared about everything that is going on right now but this is just the beginning. Those two men you saw are police officers and they'd come here to kill you."

> Even when this doesn't happen, it leaves pain and scars, and some take that pain with them into the grave. We cannot have our lost ones back, physically or either emotionally. It is up to those that remain behind to take it into consideration avoiding the same mistakes made by those before them.

"My name is Christina as I have told you before, but I wonder if you were listening at all. They claim that you had something to do with the murder and robbery that took place in Smallville. Just to be clear between me and you before I defend a guilty man, did you had anything to do with the murder or the robbery that took place in Smallville?

"Murder! I don't even know the place you are talking about and I had nothing to do with any murder or robbery in any case. As far as I know myself, I am even scared to kill a cockroach." Mark replied with a loud voice.

"Don't be afraid, I am here to protect you from them, still, they serve justice on a cold plate. I need you to trust me and do exactly what I say." Christina calmed him down.

Christina drove mark to her apartment to provide a place for him for a little while as she was solving the case. The suicide of a police Officer Petrus Mduduzi led her to the murder of the former sergeant Joey Moore. This murder started revealing the very same corrupt law that she took an oath to serve and protect. Only those considered weak are victimized by those that should protect them.

On their way to Christina's apartment, she enlightened Mark about his situation. Although, she encouraged him to keep his head up high even if the road gets harder. She was not going to give up on him. She recommended Mark to stay at her place in the meantime.

Mark kept on insisting to help out. He was eager to play his part to earn his freedom because the law had failed him. Christina took one of Neil's pictures and proposed that Mark should start following Neil and taking pictures with the people he meets in every corner.

Sometimes life is cut short at an early age from a foetus to an infant and from an infant to a teenager. When an infant die, no one blames an infant or maybe an aborted foetus in rubbish cans wrapped with newspapers or plastics. The blame is thrown around women. Those women blame men for refusing to step into the responsibility circle.

In that way, Christina would focus on the two Detectives that had somehow exposed what they actually stood for. Two officers hid something about Neil and they were not revealing. He was not totally off the hook. Christina made some assumptions that soon or later Detectives were going back to Neil for further business. Birds of the same feathers flock together.

THE WHOLE KTMG CREW sat down, as they were watching their new video on a popular television show. This was such an amazing moment for them. They all watched the video, life had changed as they knew it. None of them doubted the blessings as they could clearly see them.

The new music group had beat out the competition in the eyes of the world. They had spent the whole day looking at how the video was streaming.

Happiness is a goal but millions first, they are willing to pay the price for it, even if that has bigger consequences. "Live fast and die young".

Mhazi celebrated the success of his friends hoping for his to come. A product of ghetto-bred capitalist mental coincidentally dropped out of school. A hustler the world had ever seen, a corrupted young mind with a primary concern of making a million.

HE DIDN'T KNOW what freedom meant until he spent time behind bars. Music was the only thing between him and going back to crime. In each case, going back to criminal activities was not an option. The first step of living a better life is leaving the past behind.

> Who takes the guilt just to settle the differences? Above all, it is a question above morals because only by divine intervention all people will set aside their differences and learn to love unconditionally. The moment that imperfection is accepted as perfection it clarifies the meaning of a sin.

Neil enjoyed that his company had finally taken off the ground. To have such huge deals, they had to be influential more than other recording companies. Neil was certainly sure opportunities are fought for. Since the day that he was released from prison, he learned that money never bought respect.

Christina urged Mark to avoid compromising himself in any difficult situation because his life depended on it. Mark remained surprised that Neil was a hard-core criminal. For him to tell Christina that he knew Neil personally, it was hard. He had his camera for work and nothing else mattered than to dig deeper into Neil's life.

The two Officers waited for her at the station early in the morning. They were as furious like a desert wind with their faces looking absurd ready to take her out. When she walked into the office to drop her reports, she wanted to surprise them by letting them know that the case was off her hands. The storm begins to brew.

"I have come here to drop my last reports, I am leaving the town," she said.

"Why are you suddenly leaving? We haven't yet closed the case; the young man we were suspecting ran off. Right now, we are having his name on the most wanted list and because you have such a good skill in hunting, please stick around and help us with this.

IN SHORT, EVERYONE IS a criminal in the sense that everyone is a sinner. As much crime might be separated into two, infractions and misdemeanors the difference between the two is none because they are both crimes, and as people naturally we have failed to stay away from sins. Self-justification has failed to resolve peace amongst all people.

That is only if you do not mind though," the other Detective said.

Christina replied, "If you guys need help, I will stick around and I am not in any hurry."

Detective Anotida replied, "thank you, the more we are in this, the more this case might be closed as early as possible." These three separated ways and went back to their other commitments.

'Fame, millions and fast cars are the definition of success to everyone, old or young. It is the purpose of these low lives.'

A WEEK PASSED AFTER NEIL'S music video had been launched. Neil received a call from his mother on a Saturday night at about 21H00. They were in a club and he did not answer the call. He left some famous people hanging, especially those that wanted to take photos with him for the sake of their own images. He excused them and walked to a toilet. He called his mother back after he thought some-how something bad had just happened.

"Hello, Mama," he said.

She replied, "yebo, how are you?

He then said, "Ma, I am really busy now with work, can I call tomorrow?

She replied, "Okay, but I want to know if you are coming to church tomorrow. I want to tell you something important."

"I will see, Ma, if I am not tired of course," he replied, and he dropped the call to entertain his new friends. Many in the club were asking him about his life story. He was in the spotlight with all the money. Some women Neil considered rich, beautiful and extrava-ganza were approaching him with only evil intentions.

It is true that some people spend time in prison because they didn't have enough supporting evidence. They never committed the crime. It is such a story of two inmates that had to work in a prison kitchen only to earn 60 rand each month, with this money they were able to print files that a lawyer had to present to the Judge. They'd already served time behind bars after wrongfully accused.

This was the first big show they had been invited as special guests in front of other rich and famous people, everything had to be perfect.

It was now or never, and he proved to be worthy of the spotlight. Once again, he had demonstrated to his rivals that the game was in his pocket.

Afterward, they performed about three other songs with the whole crew on the stage. However, Neil walked away earlier than expected after facing a terrible strong headache, everything was blurring.

Once upon a time, a civilization of people made businesses by selling people and weapons to support wars. History written in the sky could never be burnt down, when another civilization raises another one falls, this is the way it is and always will be. As long as we are defined by our roots, the shame is in the struggle to understand the roots. Africa has all the minerals and resources that are needed by other continents except Africa, but for that reason, people in Congo mining areas will always suffer until the governing system has clear goals.

Unaware of the cause, he had smoked many drugs as well. It was extremely bad that he left the place and went home. It was the same night that he appointed Mhazi as the vice president of the company. He could not but admire Mhazi's tenacity of a purpose in the face of the most disheartening failures. Mhazi finished the after party performances as others were already tired leaving the stage one by one.

Mhazi performed almost his whole new album until the club was empty and closed. Every opportunity that he got to perform or do more for his talent to improve he did it with a passion. When others were enjoying girls and booze, as for Mhazi, he was working to put food on his plate.

Mhazi developed a principle that, if he came to the club single, he also leaves single. It was this principle that made him the best choice for the vice presidency in the company.

EARLY THE NEXT MORNING, the headache was still there and Neil drank all types of pills to stop it. He switched off his phone to avoid disturbances and social media entertainment. His mother tried to call him that morning to verify if they were going to meet up at the church. Neil's phone was off, so his mother phoned Tammy.

As usual, Tammy failed to read the signs that something was off with her boyfriend. She brought the phone to him and woke him up. He told her to leave, and Tammy told his mother that; he was ignorant of her needs.

It is a question of thought, why is it that a president becomes very wealthy when his people are suffering?

A parent strike a child with a rod not because of hatred but out of love. That is another way to correct a child. If a parent becomes too sweet to punish a child, the government is going to punish that child when they are adults at some point. The government's punishment is severe. Usually, they are sent away into prisons or are murdered on the way there. Some folks only change for the better when they learn life the hard way, but others change for the worse adapting to their living situation.

Chapter 09 - A Resilient Mother

He managed to wake up on a Sunday morning. He arose at last, dizzy, with the vortex of impractical suggestions revolving in his mind. Tammy suggested to him a close-by hospital. Instead of using his car, it was just too much work to drive a vehicle. After his phone had just gained about fifteen percent of power, he called a taxi to collect him. This marked his first time to have a headache as painful as a toothache. He wondered how it started. When the taxi was on the way to his house, he then cancelled the trip.

He called Mhazi to come over to his house with some marijuana as he thought that was the foundation of the problem.

TODAY'S WORLD FOCUS IS on the development plan and other things of human nurturing follows last but are these true developments? What if human life can be shut at any time? We have a better chance to learn more, develop spiritually and intellectually. However, as soon as I mention God or Jesus Christ, some believe and some do not believe because of arrogance or ignorance.

Mhazi slept at the studio while working on a duo, after leaving the club. He received a call from Neil and left some unfinished work. He went and bought some marijuana, Neil's house was about thirty minutes away.

MARK took pictures of Neil at the club. When Neil Hadebe went to his house, Mark went to Christina's house. Mhazi and Hadebe went to sit at the back yard, "Since last night I am still feeling that headache, and it's very terrible," Neil said. Mhazi sat down close to Neil while sharing a cigarette.

He replied, ''have you tried a hospital, or some sort of pills and a very long sleep." Neil responded, "I will try that, but I must be sure, otherwise when you go to a hospital, you are likely to come back sicker than before."

WHEN THEY STARTED SMOKING together Neil asked Mhazi a typical question, "do you want to progress with this music thing bro? Or let me rephrase that question; do you believe in this music business that it is going to work for you?

Mhazi replied, "brother, if I had another option or something worth doing than this, I would be doing that now, but I bet my life on this thing. It is just a matter of time before I start busting speakers. I am ready to put down the grind it is worth it."

> We are told about a man who gave it all to save everyone, but still, we deny this because of different reasons. People have been living and they are still going to live after this generation, we should not leave in fear of death. In this short life, every hero die, every poor man die, every pastor die, every woman die, and even a child die. Yet, we spend time searching for what is beyond this life.

Neil motivated his friend with beautiful words.

A friendly Advice note:

'Just remember to put God first. Happiness is the reason why we work so hard. Besides, I promise you this, you will be rejected, laughed at and even to the point that everything will seem as if it is falling apart but as for you take courage and remember that criticism will rise like a pack of vicious wolves ready for war.

Remember that sometimes, it might seem like you are the only one going through such a miserable time but keep your head up, remember boys don't cry. You are just another dreamer to them, never trip or fall down. Just raise your shoulders up high and continue as nothing happened. Also remember, it is often that in the darkest skies is where we see brightest stars, following a sunny day.

Some will call you names and tell you that turned away is all you get, just hold on to the end. Because in the end, hard work is like pregnancies that have no faults and only comes with pain just to give birth to a new life. The same pregnancy might come as early as a premature, but that is the working of God.'

> Those who wanted to change the world died and those who supported the oppression of others also died.
> Alexander who wants conquered nations at a very young age also died young. Nothing is worth living for if eyes cannot see what is beyond death and what matters most in life. When someone dies people usually grieves out of love, pain, and anger.

Neil asserted, 'Non-believers will even pray just to see you fail and fall, never surrender it is only about the faith you got. Take all the money and sacrifice it in your ideas, music, concept, and theories. If you lose it, remember what doesn't kill you makes you stronger. If you think the studio is your way out, then invest all your strength in it. Don't ever stop, just push until you hit the top.

And if you ever drop at least you will know you gave it all. Be true to yourself, in that way you can never fall. Finally, beware of these backstabbers it is not a joke that they hang around you, just to watch you go broke, just stay true to you and believe nothing is bigger.

As for me, I made the wrong choices and those choices at some point have consequences. Maybe not today or tomorrow but everything we do either positive or negative has a certain impact on us and our lives.'

Mhazi smiled and said, "Boy, when we were in prison, you were not this wise. Now, look at you, running a recording company and making deals with other companies."

It is a journey that no-one can ever prepare for, even those that are ready to die in words are usually not ready to die in flesh. True change comes from the inside, a new pair of clothes or a new car does not reflect any change. A change of heart and mind is true growth. Most people spend time acquiring information into a mindset that we hardly concentrate on what the mind can give us. Focusing on unleashing the ever goodness inside of people might be the true wisdom because even faith and love comes from within.

"You just gave me the advice of life, thank you for that. You had my back when I had nothing, and you still got my back now. We are going to make this work no matter how many obstacles we will face on the way. I appreciate everything. This has grabbed my attention away from all the pressures of life, maybe by now, I would have been thrown back into the dungeon."

Neil replied after they had just finished smoking. "Learn to believe in yourself. That is what brothers are for, sometimes we might not be perfect but nothing is worth more than our brotherly love. The reason why the world is in the mess that it is in today, it is because brothers do not love one another."

Neil and Mhazi ended their conversation. They went inside into the house to eat breakfast. Neil's headache was still there, and it had eventually intensified that he did not eat his food. He went into the shower. Mhazi remained eating on the table and by the time that Neil came out of the shower, he went straight to bed.

We also decide the differences between positive and negative. When I was freed from the chains of this life, I thought freedom was everything. I made a decision out of pride and that lead me astray into hell to burn. Prison sometimes is good that we find ourselves in our greatest times of desperations, but if we escape those desperations, we have avoided the spiritual richness and we exchange it with financial freedom.

The police officers had again visited Joey's wife and revenge was in her best interest. While they were discussing the issue, she was upset that one of the people who helped in the cause of her husband's death was still out there.

She wanted blood, an eye for an eye. The very same old way that followed her husband until it finally caught up with him. "We are sure that by the end of this week, all you have to know is that your money is being put into good use." One of the officers said. And they convinced her that the mission had become a little bold, so the payment was about to increase.

"If you do not handle it this week, I am calling this off," Lisa said. The pain she had was hurting her day and night, instead of letting it go. The death of her husband caused pain and pain ratified the need for revenge. She thought about it over and over. It was a traumatizing moment. She drank no beer, but wine, to dispel gloomy thoughts and the temptations of desperation.

A broken-hearted woman living in a lavish home of pain, instead of joy, a woman searching for anything to fill in an empty space in her heart. Nothing could be compared with the love she had for her husband.

Foster spent the whole day doing a survey and tracing the death of his cousin. He went to the Police Officers that were working on the case. He presented himself as Joey's former partner. They believed it.

These officers thought of introducing Foster to Christina, but it was a disadvantage to them. They told him about a suspect and showed him the picture of Mark.

Many lives always turn out less close to the plan, but it does not mean do not stick to the plan. Each day someone loses a loved one, and that cannot alter the lives of those that are still living in strength and health. At some point in life, we are all going to die and a new complete generation is going to be born. Are we an exemplary to the next generation with our international relations?

"This is the young man that helped in the murder of our lovely sergeant," one of the officers said.

"Have you investigated him already? Foster asked.

"Everything checked out and I am telling you this is our guy because right now, he is on the run. Since the day we visited him for questioning, he panicked and ran off like a lost dog," the officer replied.

"ANY CRIMINAL RECORD or something relative that can assist us? Foster asked diligently, but the officers replied rapidly with a picture of Mark.

"This is the picture of the young man; I can make you a copy so that you can do a follow up. These Officers knew exactly what they were doing, it was sending a killer to do their work. It was as if they cared to get this work done. They hated their own jobs and disregarded doing the right thing.

Foster traced each and every move that these Officers had made.

He hardly believed their words. The hidden agendas were clear.

It is true that crooks in the blink of an eye can recognize each other. He wondered why they side-tracked his questions." He did exactly the opposite of what they had said, he started looking for different answers.

> Death should be an example of a good character, either a person dies at ninety or twenty-five, the differences is what was completed at ninety might be completed at twenty-five. In conclusion, we rather die young to free minds that are imprisoned in slavery than to live a long life up to ninety causing a burden and pain along the years.

Neil after smoking cigarettes and drinking all kinds of pills hoping that his headache would soon end, that was just the beginning of his problems.

He went to a hospital three times a week and only medication increased.

"I might die from this," he jokingly insisted. The third time he visited the hospital, the best advice they gave him was to go to a specialist after a few nurses failed to find the problem. He went to a doctor that someone had referred him to.

When his mother heard he could not make it to the church because of the headache, for a moment, she was worried so much that only her prayers, faith and hope could save her from all the depression. The pain of a mother could never end, the only way for her to rest would be in her grave.

Neil arrived at the hospital in the morning, a nurse started taking his details and accounts of his health situation, and she took time writing these things down. He sat down for a little while when the doctor was running late. They went into another room and started doing all kinds of test on him. She asked him out of concern, "Have you ever tested for tuberculosis?

> In this life that we are living in, many people have lived before us,
> educated and non-educated, blind and non-blind, holy and unholy.
> All kinds have passed through the face of the earth after all nothing
> has changed only the characters, disciplines and attitudes have con-
> verted human behaviour.

"No" he replied.

She asked this after recognizing that he was constantly cough-
ing.

"You haven't tested for HIV and AIDS as well right?

"No, I haven't been tested for that," After he answered this question, he became tense.

He had enough money to provide for every medical bill. She took
her time to find the right problem. He came in with a headache
problem, but after she tested him for tuberculosis and HIV and
AIDS, the results were clear. His tuberculosis was patent for quite
sometime.

Neil suspected that he contracted TB while he was in prison.
She came and gave him his results in a brown envelope, it was dis-
appointing for her to tell such a young man that he had HIV and
AIDS. The doctor came in and tested him further.

The doctor told him to change medication. Neil did not take all
this well, crying about it was just another thing. In his thoughts,
he positively motivated himself but it was as if he was avoiding the
problem.

The doctor had other patients to attend but he sat down with
Neil first and gave him few words of courage:

"This does not mean your life is over or you are going to die, this
means you have to be stronger than you used to be. Go home and

take care of yourself. You are so young that you have a bright future in front of you," the doctor said.

Neil Hadebe placed these words into his heart. They scheduled up for their next meeting. Neil left the hospital reflecting on all the decisions he ever made in his life. With nothing to hold on to, he thought of blaming his girlfriend for his health issues. He arrived home and shoved the test results in an envelope at the back of a four plate stove.

> Education should be a part of everybody's life, just like how food and water is a necessity to the body, but wisdom should be above education.
> WISDOM IS ABOVE everything in this world and it is limited to certain individuals. However, the education system is based on making life easier. Mostly, it teaches things that are only useful to three or four people because still today few understand faith beyond words.

He was patient with selling diamonds, but not long after finding out he was positive. Nobody had to know about his health including his own baby mother. He found the people to talk to, and everything seemed well planned.

His new plan was to forget all his worries including medications from the doctor, it was time to sell the diamonds.

MARK COULDN'T REST, AND everything seemed remarkable for him. He thought of himself as a natural journalist. He used a car that Christina had organized for him to move around. At times, he drove closer to Neil Hadebe's house, he parked from a far distance. Nevertheless, Neil's mother hardly visited him, but for a while, she couldn't rest.

It was hard to fall asleep whenever something was wrong with her children. Tammy provided a lift for her. His mother decided to sleep over. On the other hand, Tammy went into the kitchen to prepare a meal.

> Faith only requires assurance that it is possible, then it happens through action. Education teaches about stages and hierarchies of everything, but wisdom gives assurance when everything is inevitable.

She was in the middle of preparing a meal when she noticed the stove had moved further to the front. She tried to push it back and an envelope dropped, and she stopped pushing. She pulled the stove a little bit to the front, just to be able to pick up the envelope. This made a squeak sound noise while pushing it back and forth.

Neil woke up to the strange noise from a stove and his son's shouting voice. Straightforward he walked to his mother. He recognized Tammy's hands from a distance. He paced over to Tammy and asked for the envelope.

"I HAVE BEEN LOOKING FOR THIS, where did you find it? He asked.

She replied, "where you left it!" But her concern was to know what was inside and he didn't allow that. She made a charming little grimace but a moment afterwards she was serious again.

He walked back to his mother with an envelope in his hands. She greets him, and they started chatting together. She heard his low voice and noticed his struggle to open eyes red as an eclipse, she suggested if he could go back to sleep and promised to stay for a little while for his sake.

Neil went back into the bedroom and placed the envelope where Tammy could not find it once again. He managed to hide it, but that did not erase Tammy's curiosity. Reading was not in her best interest.

Since, the time they started living together she had a great chance of going back to school, but she ignored it. As long as she had money to buy new clothes, everything was all right. Tammy was only excited when it was time for shopping.

> Mostly, everything that is done through education is the work of hands. This is the same teachings of a child to walk, talk or eat. People should not struggle to get educated and learn a certain skill because they cannot afford it, and it is not a good business idea to charge it. Mostly whenever it is charged, potentially it has almost next to zero value in the world of education.

Foster looked for Mark everywhere. It was as if he was after a myth. However, he went to the deceased sergeant's home to give his condolences. Lisa ever since the death of her husband she welcomed numerous unknown visitors. Foster went in and sat down with her. He wanted to know exactly what happened the morning Joey died.

The only person that knew the answers to those questions was sitting in front of him. He had to work out a certain approach towards her. Something convinced and persuaded her into opening up about her grief. The people that she met half of her life with Joey were a bunch of crooks and corrupt politicians. Foster looked into her eyes in search of the truth.

"What exactly happened the night before your husband was killed? He calmly asked.

"If you do not feel comfortable about it, please, I respect that!" He added.

"These two men came into this house to rob from us. After they had captured the security guard, they tempted with electricity switching off the lights. And, because we were sleeping during that hour we barely noticed that the power was off."

Her emotions instantly overwhelmed her. She stopped talking for a moment and couldn't bear the pain.

She breathed in and out, "If I do not talk about this, I will never overcome this pain and hurt. As all the lights were off, all the alarms went off, because most of them depend on electricity, it was as if they knew everything about this house. All alarms were disarmed, that is when we heard a very huge noise coming from the door."

Then what happened? Foster asked.

"They kicked the door and we woke up in fear, but my husband remained calm of the situation. He asked these men questions as their touch lights made everything blur. He could not figure out who they were. The bigger man told the other one to keep his eyes on me. This all happened in a very short period of time. The fear of death remained in me," Lisa said while grabbing a cigarette that was on the table.

> True education is for free. It is like an engineer who spends time reading and studying without a certain vision about building infra-structures and all other materials.
> Tertiary education is not the only way to enrich an individual with pure knowledge. That comes from pursuing personal goals with a mind that focuses on change.

"The emergency lights went on. THESE MEN STOOD in front of our bed with guns pointing at us. All this time we did not have time to get out of the bed. They were possibly going to shoot us in just a moment of panic. One took out the mask and my husband recognized him. They had unfinished business. Subsequently, everything happened fast, and some parts remain haze to me."

"Thank you, Lisa, you are a very strong woman and I have to tell you something about your husband. I once worked with him on a job that I was supposed to die and your husband helped me throughout. From that point, we became friends and partners. It takes time for others to be strong like you. These Officers you have paid them enough to take more money from your pockets. They found you in contempt and paved a way into your sack."

"As for me, I want your help to find the destroyer of your house, the root of all this evil." She agreed to help Foster sabotage the two officers. He knew she was devastated and desperate. He asked her about the suspects. She then showed him the pictures that the officers had brought her.

Young people waste talents away because of biased parents that are desperately looking for someone to make the whole society happy. Personal investment is a tool for personal growth. Many drop out of school, other women abort, and some get arrested in an effort to achieve these dreams.

WHEN NEIL WAS IN PRISON, all his efforts were based on making an impression. It took time for him to analyse some of the things that had changed him. In an effort to become one with his soul, he separated it into two. He reached a stage to give in or to give up. His mother could see that something is wrong, but it was painful just to condemn it.

It was taking time for a good word to penetrate his head, his objectives and life choices had led him into despair. He wanted to believe otherwise, but it was as if they was sudden lightning that'd stroke his backbone.

The only way that dreams can come true is by sacrifice, either good or bad, the result is the same. ACHIEVING ONE'S DREAMS does not mean one is happy. Many have lost their way in sweat to get these dreams to pass. Sometimes we rather cut our own hands to live better, than to be stuck in the middle of a mindless matrix. The success of money is not everything but it is something, and it does not define everything.

Our minds are set automatically to believe something through in-heritance, but the truth is easy to evaluate against lies and hard to believe. If greatness is the least and the least defines greatness, there is an adjustment that needs to be done in our human contact.

Chapter 10 - A failed Woman

HIS MOTHER THE NEXT morning woke up and cooked some porridge for his son and Neil had a cup of tea. He was feeling well to go to work. While he was drinking some tea, his mother approached him to talk.

She asked, "What is wrong?

Neil answered, "nothing much mama, only my daily routines, just that this headache took a hold of me for a while."

I saw the envelope had a hospital stamp, did they help you? She asked.

"Surely, they did help me with just a bunch of pills," Neil replied.

"That is good," she replied. They started discussing other current affairs and other politics.

> Those who gave lives to change the human mind were somehow killed, or families were destroyed. Many of us are born poor and without a silver spoon, but it is up to us to change it. Love is within us and it is up to everyone to share it through peace - Converting an intolerable mind is difficult. Belief is based on a choice.

Foster saw the picture of Neil amongst the suspects. He had a history with Neil Hadebe and the picture made it clear. Foster was completely sure that Neil might have caused the death of Jadea. Foster watched Neil Hadebe evolving from a boy into a man, it was not surprising.

Foster took pictures of all three young suspects to disguise confidence, he left Lisa with a sense of faith. The end goal remained anonymous and irresistible. Foster travelled back to the same city that Neil had bought a house. Hunting someone down was not much of a job to him. Stanley Ncube precisely wanted the information to use for blackmailing.

SHE HAD PURCHASED A gun in the name of defence. She barely knew how to use a gun, a sweet and kind woman. While she was sitting on her couch watching television she heard a rap song. She ignored it, although the voice sounded familiar.

Again and again, the same song frequently played. She saw the musician in the video, but she failed to recognise Neil. "It is generally the people that had visited," she thought. She ignored everything and that time came to pass.

> Once a person has made a decision, that person is likely to persuade others to follow the same path. The worldly view is only based on a decision, good or bad. Change requires a dominant thought, and that part is difficult because it requires effort.

Neil's mother left to go to her work after neighbors had reported a burglar who had stolen some important items in the shop she was working in. It only looked like as if the people that broke into the shop knew everything about it.

Mark spent his time watching Neil Hadebe's movements. Mhazi noticed repeatedly a car parked at the street end. He asked Neil about it during one of his visits. "There is a car from time to time parked outside, do you have community security around here?

Neil was not sure about it either. He suddenly received a call that there was a buyer available for his black diamonds. They left with Mhazi to meet the buyer.

"Lets' go get that money," Neil whispered. Neil and Mhazi hurried to sell diamonds to the dealer. Amongst those signed to the recording company, these two shared more secrets and different ideas about growing the business. Neil told his mother nothing about his HIV status.

THEY WENT TO A CLUB belonging to a Chinese man called Zheng with an average height. He was one of the biggest diamond local dealers in the area, his name around black marketers had explored like a volcano eruption because of good business. They visited the club and security guards that were on the door walked them to a private room in the club. They sat down waiting to be addressed. They arrived earlier than expected.

> In numerous African countries various societies should start producing leaders whose affairs have nothing to do with force, but rather hard work. Leaders that have a full understanding about long term economic goals. People who paved the way are so long gone. Traditions in Africa some good and some bad, all in one should evolve.

A young lady working in the club approached them, "Can I offer you, two gentlemen, something to drink? She asked with a great smile on her face.

"I will have some whiskey with some ice," Neil said.

"Me too, I will have the same thing," Mhazi shouted. Afterward, Zheng walked in with a gentleman referred to as the buyer. A retired police minister had his hands caught up in this business. This man belonged to unofficial government elites, people calling shots behind curtains. They all sat down on couches in a private room. The waitress walked in with Neil's order. They'd to do business first before celebrating.

NEIL KNEW HE COULD trust these men into a good business deal, he took out the diamonds, and placed them on the table. Zheng's job was ensuring that the diamonds were original. Zheng took out a magnifier and touch light. He took the diamonds out of a plastic. He saw these diamonds. "I recognize these Zimbabwean and Congolese black diamonds are rare to find," Zheng said.

He took them one by one checking if they deserved some large payments. He switched on a touch light and magnified every corner of the stone. He then lastly took a scale and weighted all of them there at once. He was happy that the buyer was interested. Zheng grabbed the plastic again and wrapped them inside.

> The engineers do not have a platform to build infrastructures in their own communities. It leads back to the economic crisis and political parasites. It is one of the things that could be thoroughly discussed in making the continent a land of opportunities and a land of peace. Firstly, besides poverty and everything that follows, will do anything for peace.

Zheng asked them, "Is this all you have, I will need more in the future." Neil did not reply.

The buyer had a big silver briefcase with money. He passed it onto Zheng, and he placed it on the table. Neil took the briefcase and opened it, double checking the money. He was concerned about how much money was in the case.

He calmly checked the bills properly. He knew it was going to be enough for him to be considered rich among the rich. It was everything that he ever wanted. The transaction was complete. NEIL

AND MHAZI STARTED DRINKING some whiskey with their case next to them. About thirty minutes passed, they packed what belonged to them and left. They'd a lot of money in the case, and it was risky to walk around with it. Mhazi took the bag that he had and placed the briefcase inside. They trusted nobody because of money and nobody trusted them around money. Neil went into the car and drove off without hesitation.

> Intervention is through accepting the fact that every country has its own political issues and religious issues, it is up to the leaders to sit in one room and start discussing solutions instead of problems. We have a disastrous future if the education is not extended to true values and meanings which are not just "earning incomes". It is today's smallest investment that is tomorrow's biggest business.

Another discussion started hitting off after the transaction was done, "These two are still way too young to have such diamonds, where do you think these came from? The former minister asked Zheng.

"You know one thing about these diamonds, they are everywhere, and they are nowhere at the same time. These young people are playing dangerous games. It is by luck if they even reach the age of twenty-five," Zheng replied.

Mark followed them into the club although he avoided taking photos. He really had everything close to him, but some part of his heart wanted this dirty money these boys had made.

Foster spent time checking up about Neil's life. A tremendous success, Foster never assumed Neil would be capable of success. In his mind, he had a different picture of Neil. It came to his surprise that Neil survived all his battles. The money they'd made in a very short period through Jadea made Foster a bit envy.

Although he was not focusing on this, Foster's business was influenced by the same education his own father had enforced on him.

He had a bachelor's degree in accounting. The social order affected him badly, perhaps his friends were gangsters.

Some people still must learn to earn a living, yet we are not educated for freedom, and misinformed freedom is slavery. Somehow, roots matters not, history is written by bitters, but the future is for everyone. It is important that a leader should be someone who serves everyone above himself. Be it is a leader for peace, leadership is taught in our homes before expressed to the world.

In the car, they opened the briefcase. "This is a lot of money and I want us to spend it extravagantly," Neil shouted and giggled.

Mhazi replied, "that is why I saw you having some headaches a few days back. This is a big deal, so what happens now?

"They thought we were living before, but we are now going to live properly as we should, we can buy life. We celebrate while they work," Neil replied. Two young people were overly-excited over money and how easily they had made it.

"This is all we ever wanted, making money!" Neil added. As wild as it was for them, Mark followed them with a deeper curiosity.

For these two, Neil and Mhazi, they discussed counting all the money from the buyers at a hotel. Mark only saw them going into the building and wished to follow them inside, but his bank card had been apportioned to boundaries. He paused outside the hotel analysing how organized these two were.

Foster located and visited the place Neil was living, and he rang the alarm at the main gate. Neil was still at the hotel putting money into plans. It's all about expanding and making it bigger than life itself.

Poverty childhood motivated their ambition. While Foster was walking into Neil's yard. Tammy and the child were alone home.

"How are you, Sir? The silence broke. Foster replied, "I think I am lost, is this house number 478 drive."

"Yes", she replied, "it takes time for others. How can I help you? Foster stepped forward and greeted her. They started speaking in a local dialect.

He asked about Neil, but before she answered that question, she also wanted to know more about Foster, "who are you, first? She asked. "My name is Stanley Ncube, but you can call me "Foster". I am here because I need Neil Hadebe's help."

She replied, "I wish to help you, but he is not around. Maybe I can call him to meet you." Foster replied, "That won't be necessary to disturb a man at his work. If it takes his time, then it has a value to him."

> So, People do not have support for all these types of individuals, a leader of a culture should use it to cultivate others. The entire land is filled with hypocrisy. Endlessly, we are bound together because we are brothers.
> Jesus Christ until to this day his teaching hasn't been fully expressed by any sort of leadership. His name has been dragged through the mud by ambitious men and women.

Foster wrote his number on a paper and gave it to her. She was going to give the number to Neil. She kept the number on top of the shelf and she started watching television sequels. Neil and Mhazi calculated the money into new investments.

Neil agreed to cut Mhazi twenty percent of the share. They had thirty percent of the money into the business. The last fifty percent belonged to Neil for his emergencies. Out of this, they thought to be bright and intelligent.

They packed up everything in the hotel, whilst Mark was waiting outside Christina called him. "Come back here, I have something that we need to discuss, exclusively new details that I have just received. There is something that you need to know, and you need it now. Get out of their way, before the bad wind blows your face off," she said.

"You should let me reach out and see what is happening out here. This is big," Mark replied.

"THAT IS EXACTLY what I want to talk to you about, it will not take your time," she said. Mark listened to her pure intentions, so he focused on what matters most. Mark drove back to Christina's apartment as quickly as he could. She cared enough to tell him the truth and then used him as a bait to get her truth.

Mark arrived back at the checkpoint. She started explaining everything and the whole ball of wax he needed to hear.

"They falsely accused you and these Officers knew exactly what they were doing. It was good for Joey's wife, but the truth was totally different from what they'd her believed. Joey before his sudden death, he did bad business with his colleagues and greedy partners.

> If it is everything against nothing, lives are built to be different in every way. The more families we have is the more separation we have. Joining hands for unity between colours is teaching an old dog new tricks. Those are the subjects that have destroyed men and women. Nations are created by the unity of few.

He claimed control over them. Christina cut it short for Mark to absorb all this information in.

She added, "Joey went off and did a ruthless business with some-one, and that led to his death, it is not a coincidence. In that level of power, nothing is impossible. It is a matter of doing it right and correct. They made it look as if it was a robbery."

JADEA, THE ONE who was killed while stealing diamonds had been sent by someone. An unsolved case remained the motivation, rela-tively, the job was his last thoughts of revenge. He took the venge-ance too far.

Someone gave the black marketers the word, and it was up to the marketers to decide the person capable of doing the oblivious job. There is no love in the game of cruelty. The cards are only for those who pledge allegiance to authority. Neil was recruited into a ruthless criminal meaningless world.

These people hate each other on every level. Huge dreams had inspired Neil's ambition to such an extent. Things do not always go well as planned. Mark and Christina started understanding each other's strength. Jadea freed Neil from the prison to set him out for destruction.

> It is not up to one person to build nations. It is up to everyone to shape lives. Among those who are building they also face those who are destroying. It goes on and on, a never-ending warfare.
> People from different lives the moment they set aside their differ-ences, it is the day wars come to an end. One element that is found within wars is that it carries the blood of the innocent.

Likewise, Jadea's brutal childhood started during the days of segregation. Neil watched Jadea dying and that left him confused. These diamonds were not even supposed to be in Joey's house. Joey was also good in taking what belonged to others by force. His hands were ungrateful.

Neil took the diamonds to a place that Jadea mentioned about.

It was a process of snitching one to gain from another. He evolved from all his personal beliefs to others' diverted opinions. His fear to lose increased rapidly the more he gained. The power of a hidden scroll remains its secrecy.

Neil and Mhazi left the hotel in different directions. They had hoped to catch up later. For the time being, money became everything to them. When Neil arrived home there was a whole new mood waiting for him. Tammy thought he was drinking with loose girls out of jealous. She could not afford to lose him, although she hated him sometimes.

Neil after he arrived home, Tammy asked him what was in the bag. He looked at her and smiled. "What is it? She asked smiling back at him. Neil walked around the house making sure that the doors were locked. He went back and took out the money that was in the bag.

> Poor people are into wars over the question of loyalty. Rich people are into wars over the question of land portions. Afterward, the rewards subsequent to wars are shared among high officials. The same land that is shared according to favours is not utilized enough for a nation's gross domestic product.

She was amazed and yet, questioning things.

"Where did all this come from? She asked with curiosity on her face.

NEIL REPLIED, "FROM WORK and remember you once said this house is ugly, it is time to buy a new home for our son." He feared to be a failure into his son's eyes. This kept him motivated. A young adult preparing for his twenty fourth birthday bash, money was no longer a problem. His girlfriend stopped asking about it and paid attention in a very respectful manner. While celebrating, she remembers about Foster.

"Babe," she said, "a man named Foster came by to see you, and he left his number."

Neil's thoughts wandered as far as they could find no limits or borders. He realized that all the hospital news was not as bad as Foster's arrival. When he heard that Foster came, all the long-term joy was cut short. "This is another problem," he thought.

All the money was there on the table. He had enough tools to start a war and conquer it. Foster obviously had not come for war. Neil took the number and called Foster right away. He believed that Mhazi was also equipped enough to help him with such.

> All these things contribute to the financial distribution systems in this world, it is one of the biggest reasons contributing to poverty. Rights only apply to those who know them, yet, freedom is not defined by aggressiveness towards something, and it is defined by a high moral of love between brothers and sisters.

HIS HEART'S DESIRES had separated him from God. At first, when he left prison, he felt the need to change but that did not last long. It takes commitment to change for the better, but in the blink of an eye, Neil had changed for the worse.

He could not compete with the world for his own soul. For those who change for the better will live better. However, everybody bad or good we all want to leave something behind, but is it worth it?

"Hello, my friend, I knew you would call," Foster said on the phone. "Foster, is it good that you are here? Neil replied. This conversation was as hard as it could be, but heart-to-heart it went well. They did not provoke each other in any way.

"So, tell me, man, when are you coming around again? Neil asked.

He added, "I was hoping maybe we could have some drinks while discussing business as usual." Foster replied, "I came here to give my brother a proper burial and mourn him in peace.

"My condolences, when did this happen? Neil asked again. "Just a few weeks ago, can you help me bury him properly?

Neil agreed to help an old friend and it was nothing but fear. When the conversation was over Foster had sent Neil an address.

Racism weights financial contribution, people are separated by money, not by colour or sexuality.

We are getting used to the new world while unaware. This is easy to prove especially in arguments against morals. Culture is something in our lives. It gives directions and raises leaders. Learning other cultures is also a way to educate many about life.

CHRISTINA MADE HER statements clear to Mark about Joey Morish's position. He was still the Head of illegal diamond smuggling in Africa as a whole. He knew the exact people to talk to. In many cases, Joey Moore sought mines with more than one controlling party. He would cause two or more controlling parties to fight against each other in order to work with a dominant party. His connections grew to supply cartels with guns and endangering poor villagers.

These villagers were always in fear. Money and power ruled his heart.

He cared not to understand the controversial part the villagers played.

His services with her were complete. When Neil heard Foster was around, his first thought was to run. He wanted to understand Foster's mind by working with him. That night he packed away the money and placed the bag of money under the bed. For the coming days, he had a plan to stall Foster from the truth. He had also planned to acquire passports and leave the country if it needs to be.

He regarded life as a scoop of ice cream, once it's out of a cold freezer, it is destined to melt. Neil was new into the business and some people had noticed his presence. These people that he had done business with were not honest. He took the time to think about it. It was a suicidal mission right from the start.

We should not deny the truth for a lie. Change is everything, it might be the only purpose that everybody has. Change is above hate. Many people talk about love and how unconditional it might be, the only step to that is unity.

A home without morals and principles is divided. It is not only about morals but higher respect for one another. Love today's enemy for tomorrow that is a friend. Wars are fought out of hurt and forever some are in bondages that seek to destroy everything that stands for peace and unity. A leader without God is an engineer of poverty and wars.

Mostly, the things that people see daily might not be normal in many cases to someone, we are getting used to our petty lives waiting for a better life to come. The options are not much out there, many people are stuck with simple problems because they see others struggling with the same problems and consider the problems normal, and from that, we are forever lost.

Mostly, young Africans have played important roles as liberators, but they faced a sudden fall after some devilish people took chances and used propaganda on them into protestants with enough militia strength. Without knowledge of political, economic and social analysis, people are used as weapons to perpetrate violence and increasing a nation's problem.

Chapter 11 - Voice of blood

Foster on the phone left the young man with fear for the coming days. He went back to see Lisa, the former sergeant's wife. The end of the road had begun. Lisa heard that the killer would never look like a killer.

She eagerly wanted to kill this man. She understood nothing about how a person can change after killing another person. Lisa wanted an opportunity to avenge Joey. The stories of her husband's death remained hyped during media coverage.

She wondered if all this could be altered. She wanted power over those that had taken advantage over her weakness. She felt the loss hard. Foster told her about Neil Hadebe being the second intruder.

One rather dies, than kneeling and begging to see the next day. The day that sovereignty is taken away, slavery is reborn again. As long as the power is given to the paper, not to the people, more wars are coming and more human slavery is increasing because people sign papers to stop oppression and draw constitutions that suit certain individuals.

The following day Neil called someone with knowledge about visas. He had enough money to buy himself a foreign house in a foreign location. Promptly, Foster changed the meeting and asked to meet Neil on a designated location.

128

Neil phoned Mhazi to meet up with him. Neil wanted a big distraction; his idea about a massive big birthday party was exactly a good room for escape. Mhazi was to put these things together. He had zilch to lose and all this was part of the business. Neil went to market the big function on radios and in this way, many people were going to attend.

They wanted to hide their business using a birthday party. The music movement had them on a scale. Neil met up with a man from a consulate office who was going to help him with foreign papers. This man gave him someone's contact to submit all his details to.

"Will these papers be complete by Tuesday? Neil asked on a Sunday night. Since the day he walked out of Zheng's club, those people became his enemies. Some of his role models had lived a fast life and died young.

> Debt is second from the greatest human slavery. PEACE WILL REMAIN A MYTH until we learn to unite beyond colour and gender. When one woman is abused, then take it into consideration that all women have been abused. Harmony is not a base for revenge or clannism.

He did not imagine the same thing happening to him. He wanted to leave the country with a bag full of money.

This was only possible using border routes with fewer security measures. He had made up his mind and leaving without money was nearly impossible. He was not ready to lose money for a new start. Using a bus was easier rather than a plane.

He started acting as fast as possible. Neil idolised Tupac Amaru Shakur's music and life. On the other hand, his mother's safety also worried him the most. Foster knew more about him than Jadea did.

Only through sacrifices, he remained fearless towards his own fate.

The time he left his house Tammy remained behind packing up her bags and she could not pack everything. She was still in shock and in fear. Neil informed her they were to leave. All the money would compensate for everything. The only way she was ever going to enjoy all the benefits was through obedience.

Following instructions was something Tammy hated, but when it was time to do something, she couldn't sit down and complain. His mother's safety remained a complicated situation, coming up with reasons for them to leave suddenly would have raised red flags. He reached out to her, although he knew she was not going to dig his story.

> If one nation faces sanctions, then all other nations should accept the burden as theirs. When a family becomes one, an enemy's division is powerless.

These people had one objective and nothing was for free. They did not believe in any repentance and deliverance. They suffered loneliness at times and not even money could fill in the emptiness.

Mark noticed Christina struggling to settle the case peacefully. At first, he complained, but as soon as he had engaged in the process it became difficult to complain. Mark continuously spied Neil Hadebe.

Though, Neil was paranoid at some point about a car that was parked around his street corner. In his mind, he thought they might be cops watching him.

He started getting nervous and playtime was limited. His freedom had been given days. The time that many are caught in fears, they learn more fears. Someone showed him about the visa procedure and the bribery money for a speedy visa. For such a short time, he had made a lot of money to walk away from it, and it sounded as cowardliness.

At the same time, he was a selfish father building a future for his son. All he ever wanted was to escape from his financial problems. He had envy other children going to school with cars.

His mother could not even afford a bicycle for him, it was leisure and dangerous. She could not afford anything expensive. All she wanted was making her very best from what she had.

Neil's father was never around that much to help out. Since then Neil was in pursuit of a better life. He kept on thinking about his financial freedom. "I did nothing wrong!" He exclaimed. It takes time for others to analyse the truth.

His truth was that he had nothing to do with Jadea and Joey's death, perhaps both were collateral damage. He justified even taking diamonds as the right thing. Joey had the diamonds illegally, they weren't his to keep. What goes around comes around.

There was a time the people that Joey pledge allegiance to placed him in a very bad position. It reached a power point that his friend, a former Detective Petrus Mduduzi committed suicide after his family was sucked into his business, they were murdered, leaving unbearable scars. Hurt ate away his soul and it successfully finished him off with a suicide.

Joey did not see the attack coming, and when it happened, a big problem arose. Jadea wanted to make sure Neil Hadebe loses everything in the process. He bailed him out with a hidden agenda. Friends were losing friends. Some even knew something but remained silent. If you do not speak, then forever hold your peace.

Men without quality morals are full of errors and errors leads to self-destruction. A snake remains a snake, even if the colour is changed and wheels are turned. People in Africa and the rest of the world, should not avoid confronting their government and ruling class on several issues, if it is not done properly, the wheels are quick to turn.

When Neil arrived home, Tammy was all happy. She was sure that he had handled all the business. After spending time with him, he was never going to leave them starving. When everything was done for the night, he started going through his phone messages and one message precisely. Mhazi had sent him a message. He had found a place to control business privately.

Mhazi wanted to launch his album in the middle of a crisis. It was time to demonstrate his grind. They contacted continuously for further information.

SUNRISE, NEIL WOKE up and did his daily routines. The same day, he had scheduled a meeting with a doctor. He remained unruffled, two hours after six in the morning, he drove to see the doctor. All the way, Mark followed him. It was also time for him to openly start fighting for his life. Neil continuously hid the envelope. He couldn't hide his HIV secret away forever.

> Human beings are the same and will always be. The manufacturing of guns and farms of drugs brings more income in some country, many developed countries suffer from streets drug lords extending to other crimes beyond, but for those countries with excess to natural resources, they are unaware of the benefits until that independence is swept away by a broom.

The meeting with a doctor lasted a few minutes. The doctor advised him to remember the importance of faith and patience. His life had a purpose and a huge one. Neil was on his way out of the hospital when Mark ran into him like a coincidence.

"Ey Bro," from a distance he called out.

Neil stopped to check out who was calling him. Mark walked closer and said, "I remember you? Did we meet the other day at an event? Neil stopped and paid attention to Mark.

"Yah, I do remember you," Neil replied with a loud voice.

"Jadea introduced me the other day to you. I saw your music video, congratulations on that," Mark carefully engaged in a conversation with Neil.

Leaders should be aware of their purposes. Many issues should not be hidden but revealed so that people can find a way to move forward. The future belongs to those that open their eyes while others are asleep. When the power of attraction releases energy, it brings us close to our work.

"Are you still doing photographing? Neil asked again. Mark answered him walking Neil to a hospital park. "By the way, are you sick? Mark asked.

"You are asking a lot of question at once dude, this is not an interview," Neil responded, "before I forgot, tomorrow we are having a party at the rooftop. I was wondering maybe you can come through with your girlfriend and take some photos."

Mark was excited about this invitation, and he agreed. They departed in different ways expecting to meet the following day. Mark stopped following Neil after the conversation. Mhazi impatiently waited for Neil to arrive. That same morning while producing some last parts of his album and other mixtapes, Neil arrived.

"It is still early in the morning, and you are already working on this," Neil said.

"Tomorrow's party, is it a celebration? Mhazi asked. Neil could not tell his dilemma. It was not yet time to tell his side of the story.

He only prayed to see his son grow. He replied, "Yeah, treat it like a party. This is time to start marketing your album anyway."

He diverted the conversation to music, "play one of the best tracks in the album, let me listen to your freedom of thoughts."

> PEOPLE SHOULD NOT fight for existence, instead, people should thrive. The importance of it is that; it places us in one way direction. We must expose lies in light. We spend much time pointing fingers at each other. This has been the life of human beings for eras and times. The competition took away love from our hearts and separated us from our own potentials. We live in the lands where women are for sale.

Mhazi had named his album peace and freedom. There were two main tracks about his life as a ghetto child and learning about life behind bars.

While listening to the track, Neil asked Mhazi about the money they'd pulled off from a deal with Zheng. "So what is in your mind, what do you want to do with all that money."

MHAZI REPLIED, "Bro, my life has been a trail of shame and it's time to rise from the dust. I was hoping to start my own music company at some point in the future. I want to freely own all my copyrights and other businesses in the movie industries. This is all I ever wanted growing up."

He responded, "I think your own company is a good thing, and since you have enough money to start it, you should. The future starts today and tomorrow is just another day. I think, it is your own decision, but I insist we build this company from where it is as partners.

"Mostly, these people recording music knows nothing about buying shares into a company. This would be the best, it takes time, but we can have the biggest music recording company in the country."

Mhazi was listening to all this, he'd the choice to start his own company or to buy himself into this company.

He replied, "definitely, where are the papers, let me sign." They both laughed.

> We have lived like this for centuries. Unity is above pride. We should never fight because of different political views in a nation. Artificial intelligence was born in war. Yet, we do not care to learn. Africa has economic wars over natural resources and Middle-East countries such as Iraq faced wars over oil. Many still fall for an ancient tossed coin. This coin will not change until the game changes. We need to start discussing our future. The future belongs to us and future generations.

They wrapped up on the music chat and he left the studio to a rooftop to smoke. Hours seemed as if they were set on a marathon. Neil checked his watch repeatedly. A meeting with Foster made him nervous enough to carry his gun around.

His assistant called him about a woman waiting for him in the office. He specifically said, "there is a woman waiting in your office for you, she wants to have a conversation with you, but she said nothing about what the conversation is about."

Neil went downstairs to meet a woman his assistant had hyperactively spoken of. He went into his office as she was patiently waiting for him. He sat on a couch opposite her. He failed to recognize her face. "I'm Christina, police," She said smiling. Neil went into his thoughts and tried to find a schedule with any law enforcement, while she was right there in front of him.

"Hello, Do I know you? Neil asked. This face was totally new to him, but he had his ways into a conversation. "How can I help you? Neil asked. And they were undisturbed.

She said, "I do not have enough time, because the person you did business with paid Jadea to kill Joey and you have been spotted as the right scapegoat for the business. It is a crucial blow for you."

Christina waited for him to digest this. It was not about the diamonds like Jadea made him believe. Jadea took a suicide job and he completed it at the expense of his own life. Revenge led him to his death.

She then added, "This proves you are in the mud. The two police officers paid by your private dealer insisted that you had nothing to do with it, and it is only for their benefit, not yours. They are not yet done with you. And, I talked to "Foster," he also knows a true story about you. The traders bought those diamonds half a price from you towards the deal they offered Jadea."

SHE TOOK A MOMENT for him to understand all this, "they offer you death when you love money too much. Whatever deal you made with them, they are going to reverse it and you get nothing from it."

Neil thought of it. An assertion to murder was just the beginning.

> Many children shall be born, and they will witness their own world with clear pictures as the moonlight. It is hilarious that it seems like it matters not today, but, the world has the technology, energy, business and money markets, all these things define tomorrow.

He asked, "Then, why are you here since you have figured it all out."

She exclaimed, "I have no intention of seeing you behind bars! That would be a story for another day. What is going to happen to you is called survival and that decision is yours to make. Just think through about what you got yourself into. You must work with me before they get to you." Christina wanted him to know about Mark, but that would have compromised Mark:

"Just be ready to take him down, because he is not going away. I have been working on this case and I failed to put him down for years. This is the end of it, you have to join me before he takes you down. You started a very good company here, pray that it will last," she added.

Christina then grabbed a picture frame from the table, she looked at it and said, "Your son still needs you, tomorrow and the day after that." He understood the deeper meaning of what she was saying, but it takes camels to survive the desert.

She stood up and said to him, "you need to think about this and if we delay, crucifixion is on the way." He left her at the door and said, "thank you for passing by."

Change is defined differently. HUMAN BEINGS HAVE been down this road and it is leading nowhere but in endless wars. Good leaders have good hearts to lead. Africa as a continent has been represented with an image of poverty and suffering. It has been a definition of inferiority and disgrace for the past four hundred years.

He thought Foster was a threat. He had a chance to clean up his story with the police. When she told him the story with evident proof, it was hard to believe. It was never good for him to work out this alone, he murmured, "let's make it possible."

Foster wanted a proper funeral for his cousin brother, and other motives arose after he understood the reason behind Jadea's death. Neil walked Christina out of the building to her car and went back to the rooftop.

The snooping increased home with Tammy's eagerness to look into the envelope that Neil had hidden from her. She was sure of the envelope's importance. To some degree it was personal. In search of mistakes, they are found. It is something that can never change.

Neil carried the important papers in the envelope to the hospital and he left them in the car. She found the envelope without any-thing. Tammy was expecting his hospital feedback and she kept on thinking about it.

> A new civilization is born and an old civilization declines, this is the knowledge that people will never learn. God, during wars and colonization, his name was well known amongst the sovereign na-tions. God's name is not new in Africa and slavery happened in Africa. It is just a matter of time before wars erupt in the world over missiles matters.

Nevertheless, she continued packing her bags and some irrel-evant papers. Still, she started wondering about her own status, since she was never tested before. She thought about it through, after all, she never had a healthy lifestyle. This led her to have a child before her eighteenth birthday. Her decisions to go and get tested were sudden. She had a future to maintain as a mother and a woman.

Neil while on the roof phoned Mhazi to join him. Neil under stress understood that success does not come easily but through hardships.

Neil agreed to the consequences of easy money. He looked for change and found none. However, he regretted nothing like a fa-ther. He started telling Mhazi some parts of the story. Mhazi, since prison understood the world they were living had its conditions. The trauma of being behind bars was all over, and they decided to protect themselves by any means possible.

They knew nothing about handling all this, but there is always someone willing to help. When the officers visited Neil's house, they plainly said, 'we are open for business.' This was another easy way to get away from Foster.

There is a line of corruption that is happening in the world through political greediness, from oil, businesses, soil, gold, diamonds, and platinum. The only land in the world with all kinds of minerals seems to have high rates of poverty. People ignore an aborted fetus in a dustbin, then we take photos and distribute them online.

They had the advantage to host a show up to midnight with good reasons to do that. Moreover, the two officers were totally disorganized, they couldn't just pick a side and wanted to benefit from all corners. They wanted to protect themselves using a police badge, and greedy through the way. Neil and Mhazi made sure that nothing was ever going to take them down or to destroy a company that they were building.

Their goals of making millions over a weekend doing tours were closer. Mhazi called the two officers that had visited Neil.

Since they were open for business Mhazi wanted guns from dealers. He knew with enough money war was possible; he was able to buy guns and two bullet-proof vests.

Whatever they were thinking in their heads, it was just a big wave of old trends. Only the dark was approaching with no where to hide. When Neil was about to leave his office, he received another message confirming his visa. This was another alternative for him and his family, but it was not a solution.

Everybody seems to be too busy with their own businesses and that is madness, confusion or prosperity.

The concept of living and the belief of living right have been satisfied by self-righteous. Most people in this world including heads of churches and countries accepts the new ways of life. Material success should not define right living. Education should not have a profit motive, it leads to a high level of segregation. This is the reason behind conflicts and other issues in many continents. Children in schools are taught more about foreign life than indigenous perception.

THE DIFFERENCE BETWEEN the African continent and other continents is that; civilizations from these other continents worked to
shape their future using blood bath skills for the past millennium.
Mostly they never had anything, to begin with. In Africa, children
were playing with gold and it was used for trades. People were
living well like this, although they'd tribal wars.
Leopold II (9 April 1835 – 17 December 1909) was King of the
Belgians from 1865 to 1909.

He exploited the Congo Free State as a private venture and murder,
torture, and other atrocities were perpetrated under his rule.
 Leopold was the founder and sole owner of the Congo Free State, a
private project undertaken on his own behalf. He used Henry Mor-
ton Stanley to help him lay claim to the Congo, the present-day
Democratic Republic of the Congo. At the Berlin Conference of
1884–1885, the colonial nations of Europe authorized his claim by
committing the Congo Free State to improve the lives of the native
inhabitants. From the beginning, Leopold essentially ignored these
conditions. He ran the Congo using the mercenary Force Publique
for his personal enrichment.

He used great sums of the money from this exploitation for public
and private construction projects in Belgium during this period. He
donated the private buildings to the state before his death, to pre-
serve them for Belgium.
Leopold extracted a fortune from the Congo, initially by the col-
lection of ivory, and after a rise in the price of rubber in the 1890s,
by forced labour from the native population to harvest and process
rubber. Leopold's regime was characterized by notorious system-
atic brutality; men, women, and children had hands amputated for
failing to deliver their quota of rubber; thousands were sold into

slavery.

These facts were established at the time by eyewitness testimony to an on-site inspection by an international Commission of Inquiry (1904). Millions of the Congolese people died: modern estimates range from one million to 15 million deaths, with a consensus growing around 10 million.

Several historians argue against this figure due to the absence of reliable censuses, the enormous mortality of diseases such as smallpox or sleeping sickness, and the fact that there were only 175 administrative agents in charge of rubber exploitation.

Chapter 12 - Contempt

Testifying was the last thing for the reason that it was impossible for him to appear in court as a witness without being hatched on the way there.

Those under corrupt pockets would protect their donors. The killing was not an issue as long that would be swept under the carpet. A new team had been deployed to Christina, but none of these new faces were trustworthy. She also knew her own life was in danger.

> This kind of education indoctrinated in young people has only brought dissatisfaction in their adult lives. Investors do not recognise projects until these projects are successful. Many children are misinformed from the beginning. Education should be based on improving the whole society accordingly to its needs.

She had just stepped in a land of bombs. All the same, she lost many people during the investigation and most of them were innocent, assassinated by an old grey white-haired man protected with the system feeding off politicians from his pockets.

NEIL ATTENDED THE visa consulate. Mhazi dealt with protection issues. Hadebe went to collect the passports and paying the deposit for the visas. It was time to leave the country.

Afterward, he went back to the studio to prepare for the club show.

On the other hand, Lisa sorted out a way to kill Neil. She was sure it was him because Foster told her so. Fame on the television made everything smooth. The death of a celebrity is totally different from other funerals. It trends more with actually few true condolences.

Those that live to tell the story are often misguided with ego. Lisa thought about making a follow up to find Neil. She was drinking wine when she heard the song again on the radio.

This song played several times that nobody missed it. She kept on recognizing the voice, and it was not a new voice to her.

Then, it came to pass when she saw the video again, from that point onwards, Neil Hadebe as the leading artist left her intrigued. The voice and the face matched the details from Foster's perspective.

> When everybody masters a certain skill or talent, the right way is to teach it to others for a rippling effect. The motivation behind schooling in Africa or in the world is poor and old. We have many resources such as diamonds or oil, and the only way to learn more is to replace the current learning systems adopted from foreign continents.

She sat down and smoked cigarettes watching the video repeatedly. She had lived recklessly for almost two months after the death of her husband. Her ashtray was in the middle of the table while she was wondering about a strategy to kill Hadebe.

She only thought of an eye for an eye. Her mind could not settle down with anger. The depth of it was not even in her circle of vision, her mind was telling her things. Lisa was about to make a mistake because of pain.

The kind of pain she went through blaming herself for the fall of her husband could not change anything. She once suffered strong trauma.

During that time, she also experienced a miscarriage. The grievances of an old pain had resurfaced.

"It is time for people to stop walking over me like a road," She thought. She booked her own ticket for the show. She bought one of the expensive tickets into the show, closer to the stage.

If we introduce ways to extract oil and gas, calculating financial markets families will be rich. The wealth definitely increases in more than seventy-five percent of families in Africa. Unity is the only way to fight an enemy outside the family. We should become one beyond boundaries. Everyone has a problem somehow, but we should put our differences aside and start working on one strong economy.

Neil that evening drove to visit his mother, on the way, he wandered to a church. He was searching for a deeper meaning of life, expecting a way out of this diamond dealing business.

Once you bring something to a market, they expect more. Neil went into the church thinking, "This might be the last time to step into this place, I should face my life's mistakes," some decisions causes torment. The enthusiastic to become a man led him to this fate.

The influencing male figures in his life were drug dealers and gangsters. Be a killer or get victimised for not being one. The zealous of living was biased.

He went into this church at around five o'clock. He was desperately searching for guidance. Hustling for his son did not justify his wrong decisions.

There is a moment in life we get chances to choose the right path. We live a life to satisfy our desires and leadership with a wrong motivation is dangerous. Neil emerged from nothing, its either you become a victim of the struggle or you conquer the struggle.

To Neil Hadebe, he could see many other young people just like him living large. He wanted the same life. He never had a rich father to buy him shoes, so crime could afford shoes for him.

> We criticize for the sake of arguing, it might last for eternity. When two people pick up guns to fight, even their own children are going to do the same. It starts by elders for children to learn, they only do what they see. Otherwise, we are spending time focusing on history instead of the future. We have one colour and we speak the same language, which is love above everything.

He wanted a fast lane and later quits it as soon as he had made enough money out of it. It was easy to quit by mouth but hard to apply. When he left prison his judgments were about living right. Strength to hard work, but the money was never enough for everything.

At church, it was time for him to cry out for his life and for all his guilty. Giving up everything for a new life became harder. The idea of losing even a cent made him nervous. "Losing all the money would not protect me," he thought. One of the church assistance approached him and asked, "how are you brother, is everything okay?

Neil replied, "Yeah, I was just about to make a prayer." He was afraid to be open to a stranger. The fear of judgment, in detail, he walked close to the altar with a woollen hat in his hand. He kneeled down before the altar and closed his eyes to pray.

HE HAD NO WORDS TO EXPRESS HIS WAYS. ALL HE COULD SAY WAS:

"OUR FATHER IN HEAVEN, HALLOWED BE YOUR NAME. YOUR KING-DOM COME. YOUR WILL BE DONE ON EARTH AS IT IS IN HEAVEN. I DO NOT KNOW IF I AM GOING TO BE ALIVE TOMORROW. I MADE WRONG CHOICES IN MY LIFE THAT I WISH I COULD TAKE BACK. BUT I REPENT FROM MY SINS, AND I NEED YOUR FORGIVENESS. NOTHING SEEMS TO BE WORKING FOR ME, I HAVE MADE ENEMIES STRONGER THAN ME. I CANNOT PUT MY HEAD DOWN TO REST. I FEAR THEY MIGHT COME AND TAKE MY LIFE WHILE I AM ASLEEP. LORD JESUS CHRIST SAVE MY SOUL. I NEED YOU, MY LIFE IS NOT WHAT I WANTED. ALL MY PEACE HAS DISAPPEARED. I AM LOSING MY MIND. GIVE ME ONE MORE CHANCE TO MAKE THIS RIGHT."

AND WHAT SHALL ASSUAGE HIS DARK DESPAIR, BUT THE PENITENT CRY OF HUMBLE PRAYER? HE STOOD UP after finishing the prayer and started walking away from the altar. He left the church peacefully. His next move was to visit his mother's house.

It takes courage to face any fears. His love for his family created a weak spot within him and that petrified him, and further pushed him into his other insecurities. His top priority became home security.

It was convincing for Mark that this person was somehow inno-cent in the whole story. Mark realized that they might still be some-thing good in him. Only the difficulties of life and choices led him in this dirty. Neil Hadebe was born with infinite potential. Although potential without action does not bring in results.

Mhazi had made money from the deal he did with Neil. He was probably going home with something worthy of respect in the pock-et. He thought of taking a luxurious holiday, but the family back home was going through hard times because of a major econom-ic crisis in rural areas. Like others, he wished to have a chance to complete his dreams before reaching thirty years. A chance to have dreams sometimes is a luxury. Mhazi's quoted, "Life is too short."

He went to meet up with a dealer. They'd talked on the phone. This man sold him everything to start a street war. They were looting government property to individuals for personal use. They knew money guaranteed their safety.

Mhazi's family back home had nothing to survive on. City life requires pride and strength for young black males from the projects. In a city there are only two classes, poor and rich, survival is critical. The urban has a way for its inhabitants to understand the unfairness that unfolds in a city. Life in a city requires total dedication and many aspirations.

> If we do not do something about it, talents are abused through commercialisation. The legacy starts here. Corruption is cancer, through ignorance and arrogance humans are like an experiment doomed to fail. It is not all about the money, and it is not one man's land but all men living in it. To be the head, there must be a body.

He could not remain idle while watching his family suffer from financial problems. It was difficult to help them out when he was in prison.

With a heavy burden, Mhazi at fourteen years was no-long going to school. This was a system among all of his relatives. Their parents considered it non-religious and pagan to reach the tertiary level. They were also deprived of education by their own parents. It was as if they were losing more money sending children to school.

Some of Mhazi's relatives had other children that surely made success through entrepreneurship, but they never looked back to help out little cousins. Mostly, his cousins started fixing cars, a major generational difference from their own fathers who were making pots to earn a living.

They were taught to be free in trading and to practice an old religion absorbed into a culture that their fathers would seek wives for them.

Mhazi did everything that Neil had specifically mentioned. This was the first night for Mhazi to have many weapons in his position. The night continued as usual. He had started a relationship with one other female recording artist at the studios. During the past weeks, their relationship grew deeper. When he needed to pour his emotions out and speak about his problems, she was a listener.

> In life sabotage is a tool for somebody's success, but what is the point? It is a positive turning point for others. It cannot be determined by our senses. Knowledge is built from the foundations of human civilisation. We can produce food for millions through amalgamation.

He avoided telling her other private businesses. He could not afford to put her in danger.

Mhazi had started renting an apartment with a studio inside, she slept over more often. She adored his willingness to cross boundaries to achieve his goals. He was making enough money and she was helping him to spend it. A fun-loving and gregarious man, he was nevertheless troubled in his adolescence by thoughts of suicide.

Neil's mind was far away from his health. It was something that he was going to be reminded of soon or later. He decided to start working together with Christina, and trust was something that they'd to deal with. It was time for him to look closely into his life and start investing in it more often, or he was just going to be a dead artist who had a hit song.

This misery was a reflection of all his decisions. Christina was still out there waiting for him to make up his mind. She foresaw the future and all the potential in Neil. He had no other choices besides looking closely into the mirror for answers.

IF THE GOVERNMENTS of our continents agree to one objective, then we can build earth with peace. It is the corruption that happens in one ruling family that peace becomes scarce for everyone.
We are afraid to rebuild our relationships peacefully and when people unite, they are incorruptible. It will take time before that bond is broken apart.

Anything that could not protect his family and his new investment was a threat. He felt the need to protect everything even with his own life. He slept for about four hours and he woke up to smoke a cigarette. Around 03H00, he took time to think about a clean way to get out of this. Images of losing his family petrified him most. He had to look out for something that would protect them after his death.

Foster sat down in his hotel reminiscing the old times with Jadea. He discovered some of the activities that Neil had planned. It was not all well planned but it was just enough for him to have something worthwhile to do.

When Foster was shot because of money, he learned his lessons the hard way. Although the scars on him reminded him from time to time about his unsettled life.

Neil spent the whole night working out an escaping scheme. He had many situations to deal with. The only thought that made him think twice was the thought of his own mother. She kept on telling him to choose good over evil, but just like a troubled child, he denied the teachings of a black widow.

That morning Neil got up and started working towards his goals.

He couldn't sleep well because of stress. Mhazi visited him a couple of mornings every week before going to the studios. They were incorruptible brothers.

> It is not the difference that makes us enemies, but it is the love between strangers that brings us together as brothers. It is the moral teaching that you were raised upon, sometimes nature is like a map, and knowledge starts in our homes. There are only two roads in life, and the middle one is a disguise to the other one. The sky is blue during the day and only white when its cloud.

Neil and Mhazi brought few allies recruited to institute dirt business for them. Mostly, the rappers he had started with.

They only had a rough idea about what actually happened and what was happening, they could not do much to help.

It was the first time they had a board meeting without any directors. Neil had to set things straight by creating a board of young directors. It was all about loyalty and effort. From these people, soldiers and business people were born.

He taught them a way to grasp the whole industry in the blink of an eye. Nonetheless, they were those that wanted to be around because of money, Neil gave them no positions and they remained recording artist in the company on contracts.

Neil Hadebe took five minutes to tell them about his enemies. In this way, he gave them the sense to protect something of their own.

It seemed like everything was in order irrespective of their ages.

When the time came, they promised allegiance. A new movement from rags to riches and this is all they'd ever wanted, making a lot of money and earning street respect. Such a group could not afford to lose. They understood the reason behind the movement. The end had begun for others to prove fidelity. Neil only told them what they needed to hear.

> Many musicians have a different perceptive about how the industry
> works, and all they want to do is to live like a rapper with money
> and fame. This is a job and nobody teaches them that living like
> that takes sacrifices and hard work. It is a prolonged period of time
> that takes many different turns to the top, it is not that perfect.

Foster had sent Neil directions to meet up with him. He realized the slight difference between a war and a battle. If the police were to arrest him with enough evidence in court, it was possible to get a life sentence without parole. This was possibly a time to start acting.

When they reached the place that Foster gave them the directions to, he waved a hand at them while sitting in a restaurant. They parked next to the restaurant. At 10H00, Foster was sitting alone in a restaurant drinking coffee and other customers had just started walking in. He had a daily newspaper spread in his hands.

They sat down with him as he had already ordered coffee for one. A waiter brought one takeaway coffee. Foster stood up along with them before they had any conversations. Neil was expecting various questions at the restaurant. He walked with them to their car and sat in the back seat. Mhazi started driving as Foster and Neil were in the back seat discussing his fate.

"Tell me the truth, about my cousin brother or else I will kill somebody," Foster said, "I do understand that you were with him the time he went missing." Raising more concern about everything, Foster had seen the body and had believed that Jadea was dead.

"I am the one who carried your cousin the morning that Joey killed him, and I was with him on a job. I could not leave him behind even if he was dead!" Neil exclaimed. He added, "We went to rob a house and it cost Jadea his life, it was about the money. Jadea took it personally and ended up shooting the man, and this only ended in a crossfire." He feared going back to the place he had buried Jadea. The homicide investigation team had dug the body out. Neil told Foster about their evening performance.

"An enemy of my enemy is my friend." The issue with Foster was to know his brother's killer. Someone had financed Jadea's warfare against Joey and they'd succeeded in sending him on a death penalty.

> When gold is mined, it is not as shiny as it is after it has been purified. It takes the right processes and works to achieve purification. When a due date arrives, everything falls like it was never built in the first place. Life of a celebrity can change in a matter of seconds. A reality without criticism is perhaps futile. To understand our liberty is in understanding our thoughts.

Although this was the first move that Neil honestly did, it was not the same with Foster. Before they had met with Foster, earlier that morning Neil and Mhazi met at a warehouse. The same warehouse that Mhazi had bought to keep all the equipment he'd bought for protection. They were frustrated with a vision to own the industry, power, and money.

Mark started understanding the way Neil had hustled. The more he tried to figure out the reasons behind it; he only created a web of questions. It gave Mark the ability to stick around until he sees the end of it.

The danger around Mark had cooled off. The officers that were paid to cause damage were focusing on Christina more than him.

On the other hand, Neil's baby mother and his son went to one of the private hospitals to test for HIV. She had to wait for other patients in front of her to be served. It took them a little while before they were helped. This was the first time in her life she raised concerns about her health to such an extent.

Tammy kept on observing other patients. A young beautiful woman filled with youthfulness. A nurse called her in and Tammy held her child's hand very close to her. Each moment she was nervous she would gaze at her child. They went into a certain room. The nurse started asking her some few questions.

After that, they sat on a bed as the nurse helped her through. She could see that they needed the results quickly. The mid-forties nurse had seen many youth and adults coming in after health issues and problems, possibly nothing surprised her most of the times. She repeatedly tested her.

JUNIOR AND HIS MOTHER walked away from a nurse with HIV AND AIDS test results. She was positive and could not change anything about that. The pressure to think about it was substituted by the fact that her son was negative.

In spite of being positive, she only wondered about Neil's HIV status. She was not a virgin when they met, and all these questions were starting to worry her. Her baby father had got them in trouble.

She had a few choices to make in her life and had took a luxurious life for granted.

> Whoever has a dream it is not yet a reality until they act upon it. It all starts with one step to get onto the other one. If dreams are just dreams, then the reality is powerless. A tear under the tree makes a man weak or strong.

The history of putting strength into unity is lost among people when we ought to look for a better life without concerns for others. Our ambitions are generated from our childhood. Increase in corruption leads to a decrease in economic growth. Instead of correcting these messes, a punishment is laid upon investors by those charging higher rates on those investments.

Chapter 13 - Lovers

SHE POINTED FINGERS AT NEIL after finding out about her HIV status. Tammy wanted to go back to her parents' place, but it was not much of an option. He was not abusing her in any way that she could just leave. He had provided enough security to cater to her health needs as well as her other needs.

These hospital test results presented a chance for a new life. Her days in high school during the final years, she was out of control. She was already sexually active by then. At first, she had high a concern about using protection, but that was only occasional when she was not drunk.

> Money borrowed from other rich countries like China to Africa is under threats of mismanagement. In the first place, those investors should not be attracted to such a den of land, since it is supposed to have regional competitions of investors from its own inhabitants. Foreign investments go straight into someone else's filthy pockets.

Her friends invited her to many house parties. They were calling them 'slaughterhouses' and in them, she smoked and drank. Apparently, she graduated into organizing such parties at her school.

Many young males in her class were sleeping with her at times. So everything rested in her hands, it was either Neil spoiled her health, or she spoiled his health. This was kept a secret.

She decided to take a nurse's advice on medication, for another day. Money was just available for them to leave in Europe or America. Therefore, if this was a getaway plan from poverty, she took it. She went back to packing a few items in her bags and calling friends for goodbyes.

For a split second, she tried to forget everything, but only the words from a nurse rang in her head. She was advised with unconditional words. Tammy waited for Neil to come and take them away with him. Neil had raised a question about precedence. If it was taking chances, he could not bring his own child into jeopardy.

> It is not a vision that was seen about a hundred years ago. That vision is misrepresented by individuals with misconceptions of success. What is helpful should be supported and we cannot build a house for the whole family when the family is divided. Once we learn to work together, we are likely to gather more crops during harvests than when we are separated.

In his mind, it was good for them to go to Mozambique and wait for him there. Foster understood that the intentions of Neil were good, but because he couldn't lose that advantage. He decided to keep Neil out of the loop, and focusing on what mattered most to him. Hadebe had to find other ways to get rid of this man.

Foster had a conversation with Neil, similar to the conversation he had with Joey's wife. Foster to mourn his brother in front of these young people showed weakness, he showed them no tears. Joey's reign had ended and a man who had offered Jadea money wanted blueprints from a company Joey partly owned half of the shares.

They invited Foster on the silver plate, "A person who set up your cousin wants me dead, and I want to hit him hard before he kills me. If not, Jadea's blood would be in vain. Therefore, if you want to help us, it is not only us. There is one specific policewoman interested in this man on our behalf. Tonight, we might die in a gunfight and if you mean to help, we will bury Jadea properly and together."

Foster clearly paid attention after Neil had told him this, he respected the truth, "are you saying he got the diamonds? Foster asked.

> Someone has already planted and all we must learn to do is to harvest as one. Once that is complete, we can move on into feeding millions of Africans. This could be spread into the world. So far, many people compromised quality for money. This is not changing a motive we have towards money.

"If we hit his safe, we will leave him broke and the young policewoman will have him for dinner. We have a plan for tonight, since they are going to be looking for me, and I will be at a place that nobody can take chances, but it doesn't guaranty any safety. I can also use this as a platform to attract all the attention. This will allow you and other people to hit his home."

"I will stand with Christina as a witness," Neil said. Mhazi paid close attention in detail. Their ambition for success in everything became a nightmare. All these people under one enemy. As such, Neil mentioned that once they take everything away from the former minister, the power to do more was all in their hands. Completely at first, they were all disorganized, and they had to let go of all fears to have wisdom.

FOSTER AGREED TO HELP on one condition. If they were to hit the old man the following night, whatever they were going to get from this house belonged to him, and his share to them was only a quarter of everything. This man's wealth had increased because of illegal diamonds and dealings. He owned many police officers; it came a time that they had started treating him as if he was Pablo Escobar. Christina chased after him, but whenever she thought her evidence was ready, she would be two steps behind.

> We build not just to exist, but for those that are coming after us, one country cannot build the whole continent alone. Whatever wisdom from one's head should be spread into other heads.
>
> Shared ideas can solve today's problems. Efforts from everyone makes one line complete. We should focus on our happiness, among our people, and we can also invite those that share the same compassion.

On the other hand, Christina lost loyalty during her investigations and she needed an incorruptible partner. Marvin agreed to come back into the force to help her arrest this man. Marvin witnessed ruthless things happening to innocent cops that stood up to voice out injustice.

It was his choice either to die for the truth or to live for a lie. This old man had provoked Marvin, as they'd downgraded police work.

Those that went around after street drug dealers were proven useless in the force, instead, he was interested in catching the big fish and this was a chance they wanted all along.

Neil received a call and many messages flocked in from Tammy. It seemed as if his house had been invaded. On the phone, Neil said, "Hello. Talk to me, are you okay?

He was talking to Tammy. She constantly raised her voice and he could not hear her properly, "calm down, what is it? He asked.

This made him nervous, on the other hand, she took a deep

breath and said, "Everything in the house is upside down, why did you do this? She asked.

"Upside down!" He exclaimed.

"who did this? I had gone to a supermarket to buy some food, and you didn't come here, did you?

"Can you check in the bedroom under the bed, they should be two bags there," he said. Inside the room, debris and wreckage were everywhere. She went and gazed under the bed.

It is not only for one person to have all the joy, but the whole continent as well. Entertain visitors with music, food, and dancing, and then we show them our ways of living. The day we visit them they will teach us their own ways of living also. And what is life, after all, except a complex and intricate blend of human relations?

"Nothing is here! And everything is upside down," she replied him after doing what he had said.

Neil then said, "You need to listen to me right now. Come to the office, I can make a plan for you."

She wanted to say something in return, but Neil sounded serious with a deep voice. She was so afraid that she took her son and left the house. The people that had vandalized the house were specifically looking for something. She locked the door and headed to KTMG studios.

Neil remained close to Mhazi after Tammy had just called. They took money from Zheng's club. Obviously, the next thing it was his life. During this afternoon, Neil's family arrived in shock and in fear.

He had already prepared passports for them. It was only a matter of time before they had lost him permanently. He was sure his death was close-by, but going down without a fight was inevitable.

Courageously he refused to surrender.

His girlfriend arrived with their son in the car. "Tell me exactly what happened? Where were you when all this happened?

THE STORY OF SIMBA portrays a story of pride and that of two lions a story of two kings. Every kingdom is ruled by either one of these two lions. The other lion teaches a seed as it grows, so when his time runs out, the seed still grows to be a good king. This lion rules over the land with lions, but the other lion rules over the land with hyenas. The one, who rules over the whole land with lions understand his identity than the one who rules by hyenas in fear that they might attack him. A kingdom with hyenas is cancer in the bones of a lion king.

She could not answer all these questions one time. She only said, "I went to the hospital thinking am pregnant."

Neil then exclaimed, "Are you kidding me!"

Nevertheless, he took his son out of the car. They went upstairs to his office.

When they were in the office, she asked, "Honestly, tell me, who are these people after you?

Quickly Neil murmured to her, "You don't have to worry about anything because I will take care of that, only worry about our son." They sat down in the office, and he took out their passports. He went on to open his office table drawer to take money.

He gave her a small bag full of money and tickets for her to go to Mozambique.

She tried to debate him into leaving together. He calmed her and wiped tears off her face.

"Once the business is done, I will come and take you back again, I just have to handle this knowing that you are safe," he convinced her.

They went downstairs to the car park. He drove them to an airport.

It is not for our visitors to teach us how to live, as if we were dead all along. We choose the system we want to live in. If I make mistakes, my father shall hit me with a rod because he loves me. When a visitor stays for long, he becomes one of us. A corruptive economy lives its own people in poverty, and then it blames history for current mistakes.

When they were in the car, she asked again, "who are these people after us? Is this about the money you brought home the other day? If it is about the money, your life is not worth it."

"Do not worry about me. Worry about our baby right now, it is just a misunderstanding and the police are going to handle it. When everything is done, I will come and collect you," Neil said.

"I have booked a hotel in Maputo and you can wait for me there, everything is well organized," he added.

She was not convinced by all these explanations. A moment they could be together as a family was ruined.

FURTHERMORE, MHAZI spent time in the club arranging everything together. This was his opportunity to do a preliminary album launch. Many people were coming to see their live performances. A song "when eye" had become a hit, and doubtless it was on top of the trending billboards. Every youth was addictively listening and paying attention to these young people.

"A rose that grew from the concrete." They were once inmates, but life had other plans for them, making good music for the living. They had positive energy, and they were not overnight role models.

Only by fear, we should be humbled. Those that have different agendas and ambitions in politics should be humbled accordingly. The general idea of freedom is wide. People have lost power and more control over their daily lives. We are always reminded about how much evil came through a woman, but never in once did we ever consider that the Son of Man was born out of a woman.

When Foster received this information, it was a great opportunity for him to learn about the old business that led to the death of a detective. George gave a file, and this file contained information about mass massacres, and many of them were pre-planned by highly respected officials.

FOSTER HAD AGREED to work with them, but it was not going to be easy at the end. He received a phone call from George that afternoon. This information was exactly enough for them to start digging a mass grave.

Mostly, the names that were in the file that George had sent included the same names that Neil mentioned to Foster in the vehicle, George had nothing to lose, and he leaked the information for a reason. He believed in it and forwarded the message to Christina, and without doubt, it was beneficial for everyone.

THEY HAD LEARNED to work together by placing their differences aside, a law enforcement officer working with criminals just to bring down original troublemakers, and it sounded good. Neil and Foster had done things for money, but taking a life in any situation for money was not in them.

They agreed to meet just before the night performance. They were expecting more drama to happen during his performance. For all this to happen, Christina went on to step out of her working line to get to this man. In the message that George had sent to Foster, the information contained addresses to these people's houses. It was a good move for them. And this time Christina had made two steps ahead of her enemy's.

> After all this, that pain gave birth to salvation. We face different types of wars and they all require a different level of effort. They are many ways to make a good life including prioritizing passions and sacrifices. These are some of the key elements of achieving our goals. Just to be on earth sharing life is special. Yet, Life is infinity. Possibly, we should not be limited.

NEIL KISSED HIS FAMILY as they were going away; he waited until they had left. He went into the car and drove fast to another scheduled meeting. It was up to them to avoid surprises. This meeting occurred away from a police station, they trusted no-one in the station. Neil was a perfect witness. All it took for him was the provocation. All these men only wanted power over others.

Neil arrived at a place they'd agreed to meet. He arrived without an idea about their plan for him. Foster and Christina were already in the middle of the conversation. When Neil knocked on the door, Foster opened the door with his gun hidden behind his back. He saw Neil on the door and lowered his guard. They both joined Christina.

They sat down to draft a plan, although there was a second knock on the door.

Who is on the door? "Did you bring someone with you? Christina looked at Neil.

They were startled wondering if one of them had snitched.

Neil replied, "I came alone unless someone followed me."

Foster walked to the door again with his handgun, and Neil followed behind with his own gun.

> It takes everything from those that confuse time for money. A fam-
> ily joined together with money is broken down the moment they

lose it. You live by a gun then you are likely to die from one. A word of mouth is only heard by those that pay attention. It is almost impossible to make one believe something they were never taught.

They looked at each other before opening the door. Foster opened the door and recognized George, and another police officer stood next to him. Foster stared at them with a surprise. The last time Foster worked with George, they parted ways after a brutal fight broke out between them. Although George and Foster were not friends, a common enemy had brought them together again.

George introduced the young police officer, "This is my young brother, Marvin."

"Please come in, we have to move on," they all walked in. Christina could not believe her eyes. It was a moment to believe that one of the people she trusted most Marvin was a brother to one of the most dangerous well-known gangsters. She remained quiet avoiding leaping into a conclusion.

Marvin knew almost everything in the city. He understood enemy boundaries, some would say, "He is not just a policeman, but a bookkeeper." He had access to speak to anybody including the city Mayor.

It is only for those that are wise, for they understand that if something is called bad, there must be a good reason behind it. If we are separated by our thoughts, then let our hearts be the hearts of men. When killing is habitual, then wealth from it is nothing but a heap of skulls.

Christina for a minute thought, "if these two are related then, what are we doing here," but she reconciled with her thoughts. The enemies were those corrupt in her eyes. She set aside those thoughts and started explaining the plan.

She then said, "We have to arrest him around eight at night. We should catch him by surprise and if this works, we will have less collateral damage on our hands. This man is a monster, and he will do anything to survive."

Neil asked, "Where are you planning to arrest him." She replied, "at his home, because he is off guard there. In most cases, at home, his power is to protect. We cannot afford to miss him there."

GEORGE THEN ASKED, "What are you going to charge him with?

"Numerous counts of murder to begin with," she answered. George replied, "This one is a big fish." George looked at Neil and said, "I heard about you and we had a mutual job. Although you are a mole, it is obvious in their eyes, they will fry you first."

After George mentioned this, Neil replied very quickly, "I have snitched nobody as far as I am concerned. This had nothing to do with me until they came after my family. They robbed my house and my family is in fear. They started it, so we will end it." He was confident saying this, a group of five people against one rival. They were not friends, but they swore unity to each other.

> Some good men remain the same because it is within them and unconditional goodness remains in them even during hard times. PEOPLE IN THIS WORLD have different opinions about colour, gender, political views, religion, and all the other stuff join in to make one big bunch of fools.

Afterward, George started telling them a way to attack him. "Currently, haven't you heard on the news about two trucks of loaded money were robbed with AKs yesterday? Whom do you think masterminded the whole operation? Do not act as if you are clever. At least know that you are clever. Right now, the pressure is everywhere. His home is where all that money is hidden. At the present, police officers have confiscated a few individuals."

He took a deep breath. George added, "Because you are all focused so much, you are losing the whole point for doing this. This current issue can help you to work safe and sound, and then walk away harmless. The current robbery everyone is talking about on social media can actually help us to create a cover story."

They all started wondering what George was talking about, Neil searched for this information on his phone. Christina checked her phone also to confirm George's words. When they thought these were crooks, they were stunned with this information. They'd focused on the enemy to a point of ignoring reality.

> Why fools in the first place, usually in the world of politics, poor people want the same thing, same as middle-class people and lastly, rich people. Rich people want to stay rich or richer, poor and middle class people wish to provide for their families, but their political views separate them.

George showed them a video on a flash drive. They were astounded as well as inspired. A man who had a controversial relationship with the police was helping out to tear down a virus in the governing system. This was a point where leadership was provocative and none of them knew exactly what George had in mind.

Christina, Neil, Foster, and Marvin listened attentively. They all understood that they had something in common.

George later told them, "As you have planned, eight in the evening to attack him. You will need distractions and a bigger invasion. During the invasion, one thing I will ask is to be included among the forces raiding the house. And no one has to die."

George asked, "Did you saw this one coming? TIME HAD PASSED after they had separated into their spots. George's friendship with Zheng was in jeopardy. George had visited the club owner and a black-market diamond dealer.

They had business arguments over Zheng's clients. The club needed a new scheme to handle a vast number of members.

After a while, Zheng told George that his club was starting to fall apart because of people that were using it as an opportunity to walk away from murder. He told George that his club was losing control of the business. Many politicians were taking chances and taking over the market because of their political power.

> When politicians or religious leaders see this opportunity, they come in with different ideas that are well convincing to others. Many then fall for all these things. The only way a country functions under agonistic characters is when people are separated by different opinions, although they want the same thing. However, putting those differences aside will bring unity, peace, and love to all people. Marriage is a good example of the union, however, people remain married for different reasons.

This was the only black market that emerged during the days that diamonds had no markets for illegal miners. Before that, they used to find a man who buys them at very lower prices.

Zheng and George started discussing business. George's motive towards Zheng's business was a new partnership and a strong alliance. In this way, they would be able to clean the organization, as well as restoring it back to the glory days.

For these ideas, many people approached Zheng for money to support their political campaigns. They were sure that because of greed and selfishness, some contradictions would rise. George wanted to protect and help those that were digging their own diamonds. Their idea of black market ownership seemed greed to others, but to them, it was a way to increase entrepreneurs.

Although, most people that were illegally mining these diamonds spent their money on alcohol, instead of investing it in

businesses. At some point for George, it was about black empower-
ment. They were motivated into pushing illegal diamonds, singing
black power. Zheng and George knew each other long enough to
take the organization on-to the next level.

Fearless is a man who faces fear and suppresses it. One thing about
fear is that you are always the victim. Another wise person said,
"We should not follow the world, but the world should follow us.
We do not totally destroy our demons, but we learn to live above
them." African leaders and nations are failing to put their difficulties together and seek solution that unite and create a source of life
for the people in the continent. An eye for an eye is nothing but
hypocrisy. Skin colour was a tool to separate people, but some keep
on arguing about Jesus Christ's existence, for the sack of peace, the
way his image is viewed has nothing to do with his message.

The pressure increased in every corner. The stage was set, and
all speakers were lined up for clear sounding systems. For Neil, it
was not just a birthday, his mother called him that night. She was
the best thing in his life and she taught him to teach the same to
his own child. During his past birthdays, she used to buy clothes or
shoes as presents. It was everything for him in those days.

Time went by and she realized that Neil had grown. She left a
sweet message on the phone.

When he read the message, tears of disappointment were rush-
ing down his cheek. Regretting did not help him, but empty promises made him feel better. His assurance for a better life had been
snatched away. It is hard to walk away from a fast life. He had a
family that loved him so much, his biggest fear was going back to
prison. His heart wanted to turn back, but his mind urged him to
use his intelligence. His lust for money made it difficult for him to
walk away from it. He had many battles with his soul.

Around 18H00 the club was full as expected. During that hour, Neil was home hiding many company certificates in his house. When he went to sell the diamonds, some were left still hidden in the stove. He took them and placed them in his pocket. Neil left the house in a hurry to the club.

Music was busting from the speakers and people were getting drunk, and some were smoking in the corners and others were taking photos for posting on social media. The performance was ready to start at 20H00, and everything was set on point.

Lisa came through to kill Neil Hadebe. She used an entrance for special guests and wanted to trap him the moment he was alone. Her desire for power was to see his face at gunpoint. This was her endless burden of revenge that had consumed her and denied peace to her heart. She succeeded going through without a search while wearing a hijab.

NEIL ARRIVED BACKSTAGE to meet up with Mhazi. They walked together as a crew to the stage. When they stepped on the stage the crowd was yelling.

It was a rise to fame and love as people were singing along with them. They felt an everlasting moment with people screaming and shouting for them. City students were packed in the club corners. Some students were packed in toilets smoking and drinking syrup.

When they were on the stage rapping, Neil remained paranoid with the screaming crowd. Nevertheless, they gave fans a show to enjoy the whole night. Neil tried to hold it together during the performance while his eyes were everywhere.

Two thousand years ago people had their own issues. However, ever since the resurrection of Christ, nations, and philosophies have changed. There is a fine line between judgemental words and the truth, if you confuse the two, then everything that comes out of that mouth is nothing but empty promises. People should accept the truth and stop blaming innocent people for their mistakes.

We are a family by blood, yet we all face different challenges, we should not take those challenges lightly and place that burden on others. Europe wanted to rule the world, but they failed to unite it together. In Africa, corruption and greedy leaves families in poverty and elders in mansions built by public funds. It is something that we have failed to control because we are separated. Then others say, "Do not interfere, we have nothing to do with that."

A speech that is easy to write might be hard to read out. Playing with fire sometimes burns. Survival of the greatest came from pain, we live in a greedy world that has systems to benefit the few. Changing it requires sacrifices and martyrs. We can change the world the moment we choose to.

Chapter 14 - Together

GEORGE AND FOSTER HAD arrived at a very big mansion, they had found a way to sneak in. Their job was to hit a safe inside the house. The police were playing a vital role to distract.

Exactly at 20H00, Christina rang the bell at the gate. George and Foster sneaked in when Christina and Marvin were waiting impatiently outside the gate.

"Hello! Whose it? A woman's voice on the intercom asked. "Can you please open the main gate, we have questions that we have to ask you."

> Education is a powerful tool, but the truth is, it is not everything. In the long run, it is slavery that cannot be stopped because it only creates a few alternatives. It allows a person to gather firewood and make a fire in winter. Africa should empower talents and make it a way for its children to see the world, entrepreneurs are born out of innovation.

She opened the gate without fear. "The police at the gate! This hour? She thought. It was not surprising, most police officers were informers for the retired police minister.

They went straight to knock on the door. By the time the former police minister heard the knock, his son's wife had opened the door.

He asked, "Who's on the door?

"They said police," she replied. He had most of them in his pocket. His daughter-in-law opened the door and found the whole convoy at the door. This terrified her when they started walking in. The former minister remained calm as if he knew they were coming.

"How can I help you today officers," the man said. Marvin moved close to him and punched his face.

"You are under arrested for robbery, theft, and murder." Marvin stepped forward to make his arrest. They had to be as quick as possible.

"Anything you say shall be used against you in the court of law, if you do not have a lawyer, one will be provided for you.

If you do not comply, I will use force against you."

A war can only be won by making an alliance with a small devil against a bigger devil, but without giving it enough thought, when war is won, that does not guarantee peace between the two parties. The freedom that seems to have terms and conditions is not freedom. It is a certain level of pressure when the limitations of that freedom are everywhere and when we are bound to stay in one place.

It was hard to get him out of his house without provoking his private securities. They avoided using guns to reduce collateral damage. During this hour, George and Foster were in the house doing a thorough search.

George was under the influence that the house had a basement. He expected to find everything there. They were precise about the value of information in the house. They had only fifteen minutes to walk out before compromising everything.

They went to the bedroom and started looking for a safe. The door into the basement was located in the bedroom. George took time to study this house and it was helpful to understand both. Guns were hidden everywhere in the house.

WHEN MARVIN and Christina were about to walk out of this house, police officers turned against each other with guns. They all had face masks, but they didn't fail to recognize each other.

Christina was the only female among them. She could not deal with lunatics that would murder to protect their own interest. The former minister had many police officers protecting him.

> It is the beauty of yellow roses to have thorns and those thorns are always there for a reason. When people choose to be one, it does not mean some have stopped stealing, that will always happen in a civilized world. Subsequently, we will also fail even if we are one, but it brings in the balance of work between people. The idea to create a society of love, peace and unity go far beyond centuries, and it challenges philosophical thinkers in terms of balance in the world.

These corrupt policemen survived through the pockets of this former minister. Marvin had already cuffed the man. Clean officers were ready to sacrifice themselves just to save families from this man.

"Gentleman, guns are not a solution," he said. Three-quarters of corruptive policemen had pointed guns at Marvin.

This was a way to get rid of the devil in his weakest moment. Unusual, the former minister remained quiet as they had started transporting him to a police station without people protecting him. Several times his criminal record was cleared illegally.

During this time, Foster and George were already leaving the house unobserved. They had retrieved enough information and wealth to decline this man's power even in court. Their second plan to get rid of this man was looting the information to his enemies.

If no judge was willing to send him away, then someone without fear of dying for the truth had to do it. This time around they'd found enough files to link him to many criminal activities. His involvement in the death of Joey Moore was a major blow.

> Many people are poor because of ideologies that were brought about by oppression, capitalism, socialism, communism, and slavery, the weak to feed the strong. IT MAKES SENSE that wealth can also make lives easier. Sometimes, it is within us, a mango tree growing out of pavement. Socialism brings everyone out of poverty, which makes it a specific idea for having a government and a community production, not a government that is constructed based on greedy.

Marvin moved closer to the vehicle and it was that moment when they were not sure between friends and foul. Christina and her team stayed close to each other. She had a gun in her hands ready to shoot. The man they had arrested knew that from his death many people would benefit, so his soldiers had to stand down.

CHRISTINA DISCERNED HIS fear of death and used it against him. He paid attention to her with a hope to take revenge at the police station. He laughed while asking them questions in the vehicle.

"Two of you hold no authority that can lead to my persecution. How much do you want for your lives? Because once I am out of these chains, you are going to have serious problems," he threatened them.

And his terrors were clear, in another manner; he wanted to convince them that without him, some people would come for them. It was all true that his evil hand was ready to strike them.

They remained devoted to the force, as he tried to break a wall and cause a barrier between their goals and his goals. Christina was familiar with these tactics.

21H00

Nothing had yet happened to Neil. He was still expecting someone to pop him out. They started leaving the stage allowing other participants to perform. 'We made it,' they said to each other while leaving the stage. Neil Hadebe ran straight to the garage to drive away from the public. Mhazi followed behind.

Lisa walked to the garage and they paid no attention to her. They were chatting about their next move. The first episode was over, and they had to wait for everything to cool off and testify against the former minister Christina had apprehended.

> It should be acknowledged that all men are rulers. A government that learns to serve its own people serves with confidence. Our continent so far has no peace, food and strong living conditions. The system of new government oppression seems as if it is freedom, but taxation is increasing on the poor which is the mass. "So, if people are not aware of their history they are condemned to repeat it."

There was a woman walked behind them and they had a different impression. They thought she was one of the staff members. Lisa followed Neil to his car and pointed her gun at him. She could not afford to miss him with a single shot.

"Look," Mhazi pointed at Lisa. Neil turned around at once and saw this woman staring at him with angry eyes.

"Hello, do I know you? Neil asked.

She kept rubbing tears off her eyes. At first, Neil thought this was just another woman sent to kill him. Her tears spoke louder and different. "Yeah, how does it feel that I'm holding a gun against you? The same way I felt."

Neil realized that Joey's revenge was still on the way, and he was not expecting it. Lisa's hands were shaking. All her emotions were acting up.

Neil responded, "I am sorry about what happened that night, and I wish to change it, but I can't. I was just the victim as much as you were, and I blame myself for not acting up when I was supposed to. I cannot bring back your husband. The pain you went through was caused by my actions. I played a part in this devilish game, but shooting someone like me to take away the pain won't help."

> Every century, people suffer different persecution and greedy. Their voices cannot be heard, but those that went to war and never came back, their voices are as clear as other voices. SOME WERE JUST children in war and the pain that their mothers felt is unforgettable; other generations will never know exactly what went down besides reading it from either a winner's perceptive or a loser's delusions.

She took a deep breath and stopped shaking. She had failed to move on from the death of her husband. Neil walked towards her with open arms, and she was frightened when he approached. She lowered her gun a bit, and Neil hugged her.

She cried on his shoulders. He told her to go back home because the people that killed her husband were still out there.

Neil told her that they were utilizing everything into fighting against Joey's true murderer.

She was drunk. Neil made peace with her and left her in a car garage pondering. Neil promised to make things right for her.

He also warned her to keep the gun in case someone tries to attack her at home. Until something comes up, she had to leave with a relative for a couple of days.

They separated ways with her and drove off from the garage. Mhazi drove the car and he had another story to tell. The focus was on their destination.

Sacrifice works in different parts of our lives, it only takes one decision. When some questions are asked, people tend to avoid them, especially if they are straightforward. In this way, simple answers should come from us, and not anyone else.

Mhazi then said, "Everybody wants you dead. It would be evil to wish you bad. During the time you were at the meeting, some people approached me and asked me to be a hit man for them. Because I could not say no, someone was going to take it. Since I was the first one offered, it became a great priority for me to take instructions on how to do it."

NEIL REMAINED silent when Mhazi kept on telling him his story. They were not sure about the end of the road, but surely, they were going there.

"We should continue building something of our own, and if they come between us using such ways, we will lose. Let's go to the police station," Neil said.

He added, "After all, we have tried the best out of everything. They have set up a court and judgment for this evil man."

They'd paid people to terminate Neil. Mhazi had received a down payment to murder his own friend. They thought it was a good investment. They drove to a police station. They'd enough time to put everything behind them. All their lives, it was about doing it right, they loved their hustles and music. Priorities changed on the way.

"Because they are expecting me to show up, we have to make a plan," Neil said. The moment that Mhazi decided to go against his word with these men, Neil's enemies were also his. Instantly, they both had a bounty on their heads and running away in terror was never going to help. The police had helped them to come clean, but it was not enough to keep them safe.

In this world, criticism has a number of restrictions which is always in favour of many people but it closes the doors for understanding. Most answers in this world are from questions people barely ask.

It is just a matter of seeking the right questions, and answers are always provided. When a heavy rain of the year is about to fall, do we prepare for the mud?

When they'd reached the police station everything seemed normal from an outside gaze. Inside the station, something else was happening. They waited in their vehicle for Foster and Marvin to call them and identify the man. This operation involved a judge's warrant to arrest, a former police Colonel, and other higher-level persecutors. They managed to keep this confidential. Running the operation in secret saved many people from their tombs.

One officer was murmuring to another, "They have brought coffins in here." They knew many of the officers were corrupt, and the whole governing system had been corrupted.

Neil Hadebe and his friend sat in a car wondering exactly about the cost of betrayal. This is "karma" and it doesn't let go easily. Moreover, if by any means they were going to survive, they grew up talking about wealth, and how much they wanted a lot of it. Wherever they were going to live always a burden would follow.

These two young people realized they were doomed. Anything for money meant well, it was worth it. They ended up knocking on a wrong door for help. The love of fast cars and woman led them into a life of guns and bullets.

A recipe for a better future starts by letting go of the past. When children are born innocent into this world the process of receiving misinformation corrupts them. All these children receive history lessons faster as they catch up with the rest of the world. The separation begins when they start interpreting the actual meaning behind the information received. It is in this education that children are taught unknowingly about wars.

A man they'd made a deal with could not forgive or forget. A decision to bury him was random. Something that mattered most to him seemed worthless to other people. They knew he had long sold his soul for daily meals.

Neil's phone rang while laid on a dashboard. He answers the private number.

"Hello," he said, and then added, "Who is this? Neil failed to recognize the caller's voice.

"Tell your friend that he is as dead as you are. The moment you will testify in a court, consider yourselves dead. They are putting a price on your head. Either make up your thoughts right or we will blow them off."

Mhazi's eavesdrop picked up a few words out of the conversation. Street life was not fun anymore. Going back to apologize was just another triggered time bomb. Neil before he replied on the phone, the private caller cuts him off and drops the call. Afterward, they asked each other questions about the caller. In the middle of confusion, the phone rings again.

Children are educated into both negative and positive thinkers, but they are first taught negativity. The educators' aim is to program children and withdrew strength out of their negative emotions. Racism and hatred are born out of negativity.

This time around it was not a private number, but Foster's number. Just after that, Neil and Mhazi went into the station, following the instructions of the second caller.

They had little knowledge about witness protection procedures.

Someone took them to the investigation room which had a two-way mirror. The two witnesses went in when Christina opened the door for them.

The former minister was on the other side of the mirror; they could not doubt further. This man still thought that everything was a joke. Neil and Mhazi recognized him. After they had identified him, another man in a black suit standing next to them shook their hands and said, "The state will thank you for this." They had smiles leaving the room and Christina notified them about witness protection. They only hoped it won't last forever.

the last intervention

"Better is a dish of vegetables where there is love than a fattened bull where there is hatred."
History does not forgive and does not give the whole truth, it is only written based on the winner's opinion because history remembers all good things and destroys any evidence related to genocides. History gives governing elites wrong priorities because everything is based on proving certain ideologies. When we become a people, based on our history we share the same pain.

NEIL QUESTIONED Christina's motives, "We thought this is our last time to step inside of a police station, and what is this witness protection protocol. Can you explain clearly what is going on here? He bellowed. She then understood that the fear was not just in her, even these two.

"The truth is that you are actually true witnesses to all this and your part is big than ours. Do not worry about safety because any part of this country is touchable to their gang, so I will send you to any country of your choice, but it has to be in Africa. It is hard to find someone in Africa, only if they are into social media."

"What should we do? We cannot go back home." Mhazi asked.

She answered him, "do not worry about resources or anything like that, I will have your plane tickets ready in the morning. But if you still want to do business, I live that to your own risk."

Neil chose the way Christina had provided. It was the best way for them to get cleared from every bad record. They realized the powers of an original criminal cannot be stripped away by amateurs.

It is during this time we think of leadership, but then again it is not every time that war is necessary. When people become one and throw their guns away, they can pick up bricks and start building homes for the homeless and cook for the hungry. At that moment we lay the first brick, we start building the future.

Christina told them about all procedures as they were walking to the car. They left the place with Christina's car avoiding someone to chase after them. When Christina left the station, she asked another two policemen to take Neil's car to a private garage.

She drove them to a disclosed location. Christina treated them like gold since they'd helped her with the investigation. They spoke a little in the car about current events avoiding uprising concerns. They comprehended facts of going back to the old life as a predicament. She arrived at a disclosed place after twenty minutes of speeding.

Mark was not expecting to see Neil after the show. They walked in to find him eating popcorns watching television. Neil asked enraged, "what is he doing here? I thought this was a secret place."

Lisa rushed into defending Mark, "Yes, it is Neil. Relax, this is Mark. My guess is that you know each other already."

Mark and Neil shook hands like strangers. He accepted their problems with composure and she with equanimity. When the situation had calm, they started talking about music right away.

They were done living under the fear of someone, if it meant death, then they were ready to take it. They'd different places to sleep in the house, but it was hard to trust Mark. They watched television and constantly smoked cigarettes. "Neil that song is popping. How did that happen?

Neil replied, "We only do this for money and its only business from our own perspective. We were born hungry and this is our way out of poverty, we wish if we had PhDs or something close to that, but a studio experience is the only highest certificate we have."

The mindset of a struggle is for a soldier that needs a purpose to fight. The mind of love constructs. We are born into this world to die in it. The pace of life is becoming short. We spend more time in worries. It is not for any of us to be worried about financial freedom. We have managed to blame others for our troubles, it is only the moment that we close our eyes, that everything becomes clear, and one can truly see.

FREEDOM COMES FROM control over thoughts. We can manage to have freedom from wars, but we can never manage to have freedom from our own intellectual slavery before understanding what it is. We are born out of rules and laws. All these laws have been followed because of fear. When change is mentioned to us, at times we deny change. Many human beings have completely evolved because they refused to change. When one is brainwashed, he/she will kill to protect a religion or a cult. Religion without sacrifice is nothing. We are meant to be great from nothing to something, but this can only happen the moment we change our way of thinking.

Chapter 15 - Men at War

A s they were gossiping, Christina went back to the police station. She still had unfinished business on her watch. Neil and Mhazi asked Mark some questions out of concern. "Why are you in this place? Are you some secret police spy or something close to that?

Mark replied them, "do you remember the job that you did with Jadea, when they were investigating it, two policemen in charge had a problem solving it, and they pointed fingers at me. They wanted to bury me to stop the investigation because someone had paid them to quietly solve this case. It went off the road, especially after Christina intervened."

> Do not follow leaders or elders, but follow the message. It is only the message that leaves on. We should never isolate ideas because our feelings assume otherwise. A dream is only a dream before hard work. We must learn and adapt to change; we must recognize the need for change.

"Everything is about her and she is dedicated. She saved me, and also knows that you played a part in Joey Morish's death. These two officers avoided to arrest you because the diamonds from Joey's house were still in your hands. They couldn't risk losing the diamonds by scaring the bird away. They did let you go for a reason."

This was a total surprise to Neil and very shocking news to Mhazi Tshuma. Mhazi knew nothing about this besides that something happened to Neil.

Mark continued, "When we met at the hospital. I was actually following you, I didn't want to die for something that you did and curiosity continuously carried me away."

They had one enemy and the way forward was working together. They were all young and ready to change their lives.

> The ones we love are the ones we do everything for. If one family
> has wealth and all children of the family are educated, the solutions
> are taught to these children. Not everyone out there is as blessed as
> they are. The day children discover the truth, they shatter even their
> own parents outside.

Mark gave Neil Hadebe a camera to watch some parts of their performances. When they were smoking, Neil remained behind watching other pictures.

Mhazi shouted, "Here is a joint." Neil refused to smoke for the first time in his life and it was very unusual.

"Man, talk to me, what is wrong. This is not like you, what is wrong? Mhazi continued shouting.

Neil did not answer that. "Mark, only my pictures are in here, this has been going on for some time and I did not even blink an eye. And you made it this far. People get killed for doing this." Mhazi and Mark hung out at the balcony.

Foster and George were looking into the information they'd found in the house. An easy way to confiscate resources and assets hidden was through these files. This former police minister had buried many people alive and created enemies on the way.

Retired minister Siya was a delicate man with intentions to change a number of laws, yet not accountable for his misdeeds. He never regretted any mistakes for a very noble cause. Siya never gave anything to anyone for free. Exploitation is a passive voice to some and very active voice to others. An indefinite man cannot solve problems without using violence.

The people that had protected him for a very long time decided his reign had come to an end. They realized that life is always and will always be greater than the next person as others die and others are born to thrive. The fear to lose wealth is a prison.

Christina increased her vehicle's speed after recognizing someone was following her. She took a chance, but that made her a target. They couldn't let it go, she had declared war on them. She drove into a truck on her way to the police station. It was not an accident, but a planned move. The people that had set her up wanted her to die instantly on the spot.

> FAIRNESS IS hard in this world because we only teach segregation and the need for power. How then do we expect to have a better future for everyone? People become successful, not because they want to give, it is an ambition born out of ego sometimes. Life begins when a self created-image dies. THIS ANSWER ALSO relates to where people on the continent have reached so far.

She had created honest in the force by arresting political alliances that were victimizing innocent people. In a split second of an accident, her car flipped over. They had been convinced that they were untouchables until she came through. The time she laid a finger on this man her destiny was set on fire.

While driving she looked back and forth, another truck ran into hers intentionally. She was not expecting them to come after her like that. He had enough power to play around with people's lives.

She thought of taking advantage of a corner robot, but a big truck coincidentally trapped her in a corner. Those who saw it happening screamed at the scene. For a moment, there seemed to be a kind of commotion, a numbness of noise. Few people witnessed the incident and could tell which driver was in the wrong direction. This all happened around 22H30, close to midnight.

An ambulance arrived ten minutes later after some people had pulled her out of the car. This did not mean the danger was over. When she survived the accident, her life at a public hospital was in danger still. Honest could not guarantee her safety.

After the accident, she couldn't move or escape. It was hard for an unconscious woman to protect herself. It had become difficult for Christina to have a life outside the police station.

> When elders or freedom fighter fought against human segregation, it was something they saw and experienced. When people see struggle or oppression, naturally they fight back. Whenever this happens, people are not allowed to express freedom. They are always reminded, "We fought the war." People that fought and died in wars had more courage than those that later interpreted the story.

A vehicle that was following her changed the street. They avoided being spotted with street cameras. This was just the beginning of the end. They all saw an opportunity and dove into it.

They still followed her after the accident. They all wanted her buried.

She remained loyal to her priorities and principals, which is something that mattered most in her entire life.

Her mother advised her to settle down, but it fell on deaf ears. Coming, as she did, of a shiftless, indolent family, she was yet a splendid worker.

Her answer was, "I work all the time and I love what I do."

With so much effort in her, they wanted to destroy that good spirit in her.

George impounded the former minister's laptop. The former police minister hardly spotted the raid when all the police arrived at his house. It seemed like a joke until the persecution started.

They retrieved many documents buried in the laptop. This folder contained the exact details to prove his guiltiness in all this. This man started as a police officer and rose to power when he departed the force to join a political party. In this party, they obtained loyalty, delivery and honest from him, that boosted his career's cancer.

> A man who is not a soldier thinks a uniform defines a soldier. A soldier means courage. We live in a life of battles against ourselves. We fight everyday against those things that surrounds us. When we are poor, all our efforts are invested in making a fortune. Fuel is a catalyst for fire and a recipe to burn houses. An embarrassing insult is when we compare ourselves to other people. When are we ever grateful in our lives?

These were some of the brutality George encountered. George and Foster copied all the data into different flash drives for security reasons and dividing the information for personal use. If the information had leaked to the public, it would have caused chaos and rallies. They were already at the winning side. A piece of candlelight in a dark room can't be ignored.

Diamonds were smuggled in car seats, and the police knew these discrete cars coming out of the Marange diamond fields. George used to drive out of the fields with diamonds shafted in shoes and car seats. Some policemen at tollgates would search their cars thoroughly.

They were not arresting these people, but only wanted a share out of these diamonds. This was just one of the challenges that the smugglers were facing. When it was time to do something, they took a risk from one point to another.

Foster submitted evidence after confiscating hidden assets for himself. In this way, they got hold of many valuable items including expensive jewellery. The valuables amounted to over fifty million. One folder with files led them to the next.

They had separated hotels with George due to trust issues. Still, for the first time, they worked together with police considering in their best interests in place.

> If we are not grateful, we will remain egotistical until the day of our last breath. A bad heart is not defined by skin color, we are all good and we might be bad as well. Fighting against the truth is when we are in denial. Whoever is poor, will become rich and whoever is rich might as well become richer. We cannot starve each other because of history.

THE BOYS WERE STILL chatting with Mark. Mark persistently requested Neil to join their businesses. They had finished arguing about their differences in lifestyle. Mark persisted in offering Neil a business partnership.

He understood much about video production platforms as an independent artist, he was willing to unleash all this knowledge into their company with provided resources.

A young business male grabbed an opportunity with two hands

for making music videos, marketing, advertising, and business decisions. Mark had fully-fledged on social media promotions, allowing him to sell people's products easier.

They mentioned about making movies which seemed impossible and a far-fetched goal.

Neil sat his eyes on building a music territory in order to walk away from fame into a business mogul.

The fact that fame took away his private life into the public eye, it handsomely affected his private double-edged knife life. They wanted to have more riches off cameras avoiding paparazzi.

> We can be the most peaceful people once we eradicate poverty and allow families to produce their own food. Employment is not the end-goal, but independence to build legacies might be. Influence comes from freedom, and when we live, we must live to celebrate. We must learn to adapt and create an environment that suits everyone.

They'd studied the entertainment industry from the ground up, the focus on notoriety and nobility determined respect from various artists.

During the days in prison, he read about past industry mistakes and commercialization that has consumed great artistic talents to the least, leaving them in debt.

Mark, Neil, and Mhazi continuously debated around commercial issues. Their perception of groups and unity were political influenced ideologies. They spoke about the financial crisis, technology, politics, woman and other current situation.

Mark ended up sleeping on a couch after watching a television show. A phone laid on the table rang unexpectedly.

Marvin was on the phone and Neil took his time to answer the call, "Hello, Marvin?

"I have been calling her phone, tell me is Christina there?

Neil reacted anxiously, "pardon, and repeat again".

Marvin asked out loud with a clear sound, "are you with Christina? I tried calling her a several times and it is not going through. The last time we talked, she was on her way back to the station."

At this point on, Neil started understanding the bad side of gangsterism, always in a very negative way.

"She left here a few hours ago. All this time, we assumed that she is with you."

As he was saying this on the phone, Mark woke up from his sleep after some sound disturbance. They were entirely in fear rather than in shock, they were next on the target list. Marvin insisted to keep in touch as soon as she shows up.

"What happened? They asked each other questions without any answers. The first thing in their minds, "she went to war." Neil asked Mark with confidence about Christina.

"She left going where again?

"Police station," Mhazi replied.

"She is not at the station and they are not sure if she is well. We pray to God that she is, otherwise, we have her death on our hands."

They remained silent after the news. If they were to sit with their hands folded waiting for someone to come, then it was going to take forever. They reconsidered this decision, and it was not easy for them especially for a person that had come through for them.

On a few occasions, we meet new people that we envy against for no reason. The image of a celebrity as a god is biased, life as a celebrity is nothing close to what children see on the television.

"If she is not at the police station, then we should find her," Mark insisted, he knew areas that Christina would go.

He took a suitcase that Christina had instructed him not to touch unless it was necessary. This was exactly the right time to open it. He found few weapons in the suitcase, money and six different passports that belonged to her. Before closing the bag, they were examining her level of authority because she had them biased for a simple policewoman.

Mark used a car she had long provided for him. The same vehicle he had used to trace Neil Hadebe with. Mhazi saw the car and recognized its number plate to the last detail. "I remember this car," he said.

They left the garage to find Christina. Particularly, Mark had an eager to find her, given that she had protected him more than once. He drove the vehicle using the main streets Christina showed him, in case of such an emergence matter.

Another battle had ceased for another to start. It's hard to save one another when the enemy is indirect and unclear.

On the other hand, Christina was in a hospital fighting for her life in ICU and on the oxygen. A tragic accident left her bruised.

Though she survived, her enemies tried the first attempt and failed, she was not yet safe. The ambition for justice led her astray. Their intentions were to kill her. Murderers were still out there looking for her.

Marvin could not leave the station for his break, although the place had high intelligence officers looking after the case.

For Marvin to trust any government official, it was not only difficult, but the problems that they were currently facing had been caused by a government official. He'd lost trust in the government and many officers had been slaughtered in the hands of civil servants.

> A poem of a devil, ''Fight against all odds, destroy what is good
> and ruin families for money and power.''

Chapter 16 - A Soldier's Heart

MARVIN MADE SURE THAT his eyes were on the prisoner all night. He kept drinking coffee over and over. Nonetheless, his concerns about Christina amplified, this made him more nervous and more focused. MARK DROVE AS FAST as he could, hoping to catch up with her.

When Christina arrived at the hospital, doctors operated her in private. Before they knew, a nurse caring for her left the room for about ten minutes. When she came back to check up on her patient, Christina was not on the bed anymore.

> These celebrities are hard workers, and that is one of the reasons behind their successful stories. Just in general, hard work should be improvised. We must seek help only when it is necessary. We should learn to make sacrifices. Instead, if we follow the pattern of those that lived before us, those in the future might as well suffer the same problems we suffer today.

The nurse tried to make sense of it all, but nothing came up. At first, when she walked into the room everything was in order except the patient. The nurse double checked everywhere, until she realized the patient was missing. She had left the room for a cup of tea while her patient was on a comma.

Afterwards, she went to the reception. A patient like Christina would not have been transported to another hospital facility without her acknowledgment.

"I missed something, but how can it be," she asked everything at the reception, but nothing new came up.

Mark drove following Christina's ordinary roots. On the way, their attention was caught by yellow tapes covering another part of the street. They ignored it since they were used to the seamy underbelly of a city where everything is possible. Once Mark had driven about a hundred meters away from the scene, Neil told him to stop the car and reverse back to the scene, and they might have missed something else from it. Mark drove back to the scene.

> We must focus on those long term goals and what is worth our time. The pain of Africa or the pain of the world is increasing daily. It is like a tree, a tree that is in the middle of the garden. When this tree loses its roots, even a very beautiful fruit falls from the tree and turns sour. The tree loses its very beauty.

Afterwards, the nurse left the reception as if she was mad, she went on to ask securities if they'd seen the patient, but for a place full of patients and visitors walking in and out, they were not sure. They continued looking for Christina together.

Another building security insisted on cameras and persisted to check what had happened on the floor. About five people were watching the surveillance footage, they fast forwarded it to capture certain moments. They were concerned about her more than other patients. Some of the things that confused the nurse included Christina's broken leg, and she had been unconscious to leave the hospital.

This nurse remained fascinated and petrified regretting spending time on the phone instead of spending more time nursing a patient. When they looked closely at the cameras, some people went into the room with a wheelchair. Two unfamiliar doctors took Christina away.

While watching it everyone realized the woman had either been kidnapped in the hospital, or she had been transferred, but for eyes to believe the female nurse wanted signed forms. This nurse remained bothered that these men left the room with Christina on a wheelchair and it seemed cruel and wild.

> God in this life has always reserved a place for fallen fruits, for their seeds are the foundation of new trees. Winter comes, and SPRING blows away a new season. When a seed is covered by soil, November rains and life emerges from a dead seed. All green leaves are restored. Hope comes from attempts, and if you sit and fold hands, then hopeless is your best friend. We should recognize Africa as one.

She was not in a condition to be out of the bed, especially on a wheelchair, because there were further operations scheduled for her. She asked these security guards, "Who are these men? Literally, I do not recognize any of them." "Relax, let's call it in," they replied.

Most doctors were off duty for late hours. Mark parked their car along the road and hurried to open car doors. Neil quickly ran to see if she was still in the car.

Mark arrived at the scene and saw Christina's car in pieces.

He fell down on his knees and wept silently, only tears were determining the deeper pain.

Local police officers had surrounded the place with two police vehicles. Two officers walked faster close to them so that nobody else would disturb the scene. Neil told these officers about the car that had crashed. They wanted the right of entry to examine the accident. They all hoped that she was well and alive. Mark walked closer to one of the officers and told him about the owner of the vehicle.

"WHERE IS SHE? HE ASKED.

One of the young deputies replied him, "we have found one of our badges here. She is an officer and an ambulance has transferred her to a hospital, but we cannot tell you anything else until you provide evidence that you know her?

They were stuck, Mark thought of lying, but that was not going to work. Neil called Marvin to let him know about the accident. The officers that were controlling the scene were stubbornly rude.

> We should do it for those that will live after us. We should leave this world better than we found it, those before us played a good part and it is in our hands to complete the work. We can conquer fears if we try to, so we should reconsider our friends and choose them wisely. Do not feel like a visitor whenever you are home, be free because you are home.

"Hello, is she available now? Marvin asked. It seemed as if he was still in the dark about the accident.

Neil replied, "We have found her car crashed into another truck and it's an outburst. There is an officer here, refusing us access to search for information here. We need help to get facts out of him, she has been transferred to a hospital. So far, we are not sure, which one is it."

Marvin responded, "This is not looking good at all, give that officer a phone and I will talk to him." Neil walked over to the deputy officer and gave him the phone.

"Hello, who is this? The deputy asked.

"Hello, my name is Marvin reporting from D11-6, can you please tell these young fellows the hospital that Christina has been sent to. We are currently in the middle of an investigation and your assistance at this point is helpful."

The deputy officer replied to him, "I understand you, Officer." He gave Neil the phone, they spoke immediately about the hospital.

"When we arrive at the hospital, we will tell you what is going on and the condition that she is in, if possible we will keep her company until she is safe." Neil dropped the phone, and the deputy opened up about the accident and witnesses.

Marvin remained quiet about Christina's situation in the station. He knew his life was also in danger.

The difficult about trust had risen when some bad officers were eager to break the prisoner out. At once, Marvin walked away from the force and Christina had persuaded him to seek justice. He had agreed to see the end of the road. They knew the danger of facing an evil rich man and putting him in prison. They remained different from officers without good motives to serve and protect.

> You should know who you are. Even after acquiring knowledge about the generation before us, we should remember right at that moment, we are living in the future of those before us and yet in the past of those after us. We should make decisions that guide and teach others, failure means one-step to go. People born without anything are full of ambition to achieve great things.
>
> The world is like a criminal that drains energy from the innocent to feed the wicked. When a court is an illusion for justice, and a false justice system sends minors into prisons. A false church is teaching false doctrines in the name of the Lord. The world is criticizing a good doctrine for a lie.

Chapter 17 - The Ugly Truth

MARK, NEIL, AND MHAZI went to the hospital that a deputy had directed them to. They reached this place and everything was upside because Christina had gone missing. It was a big deal as the nurse was trying to make her statement clear to a doctor in-charge. It was as if this was just another television drama.

As they were going to this room, a security guard stopped them, "how can I help you."

A school can cover up students' abuses, in exchange, for good results. It is not everyone whose guilt for another's crimes. Each man and woman in this world has a story to tell. It is a matter of a choice that makes us better. Equality is born out of forgiveness, and success is born out of courage and hard work. Nevertheless, love is different because it takes practice.

Mark replied, "We are here to see a friend."

He then asked them, "Can we take you to that floor Please."

They started walking together. After mentioning the room number, the security stopped walking.

"Is there something wrong? Mark asked. The guard's face fell off and spotted their impression. In a deep voice, he told them, "we called the police, the patient is missing."

Neil exclaimed, "the police mentioned that she went on a comma, how did this happen? Can we please go to the room that she was in, maybe our eyes can believe it more than our hearts? The security guard walked with them explaining how the whole situation went down in an instant.

The security opened the door wearing gloves avoiding fingerprints. "This is the room."

Mhazi remained quiet until they walked into the room, "how can this happen, do you know how important that person is to us? These hospitals are careless about people." Neil walked out of the room and phoned Marvin again about the circumstances at hand. The security officer started explaining everything in detail. They had missed a point, and her disappearance was quick enough that nobody witnessed it.

> A train can be hidden by another train. Time travels from coasts to coasts as we fade away. Supporting our interest every time will not save us in the long run. The truth about inventions is that nobody is willing to participate when the inventors ask for help. Those that are placed in charge of analyzing false and the truth are key players in pleasing wrong eyes, yet, they watch and laugh as the truth is fading away. We all praise lies while widows and children cry out for help.

This hospital as a whole failed expressing the incident in few words and on behalf of the hospital, a doctor spoke to them. They were very angry, Mark sat on a bench across the room.

This was another dead end.

"Marvin, we are at the hospital and it's bad," Neil said.

"Talk to me, how is she doing? Marvin asked.

"Man, it's pretty bad, she is gone and they cannot find her. They said some people took her, she was kidnapped and we are failing to move forward from this point onwards."

Marvin murmured, "This is bad, from bad to worse, but if she is dead, we will continue with the persecution because George and Foster have enough evidence to put this horror behind bars. Go back to the safe house. I will further notice you."

Neil replied, "Why should we go back to that place? They are searching and hunting us before the trial. From now on, we will survive by our own means."

> We make to break or break to make. Nicole Machiavelli mentioned that at first a prince is chosen by everyone, but in the end, the prince is rejected. They will outspokenly discharge him with his ideas and thoughts. Everyone has a different opinion and they should be evaluated at all cost, but we should remember that we make choices based on either the truth or our feelings. Sometimes we fail to recognize the best things out of crazy things. "Isolation for a different opinion is a revolution."

Then Marvin replied, "Just do the best you can, and keep this number with you at all times. We cannot afford to lose."

They left the hospital before someone had spotted them. Fluctuation and frustrations were all over their faces. Which place can we go and hide-out? Neil could not blame anyone, but his love of money had instigated this.

He wouldn't last a moment without thinking for a second about his mother or son's safety. Neil failed to tolerate losing the only people that genuinely needed him. It was all his mess, and it was up to him to clean it up.

He wanted the glamorous fruits that Tupac Amaru Shakur and Christopher Wallace (Notorious B.I.G Smalls) preached. They believed in their dreams like him and became influential young people. They wanted to be feared by others. Just like Neil and other young males they often forget that Tupac and Christopher were murdered, the two cases remain unsolved. They both lived short lives. This was a turning point in the music industry. Many young males do music under the influence of a better future.

> Our fathers taught us about how bad a neighbor can be, greediness, selfish and evil. We believed them because they were our fathers, but it came to a point that our fathers were greedy, selfish and evil just like our neighbor. When we started asking questions about it, some of our brothers started dying one after another because of it.

Marvin failed to keep the secrets about the accident. He called George and Foster to inform them. When George heard the story about Christina he was disappointed. Whoever took her had no good intentions for her. During this hour, George mentioned to Foster about many people that had disappeared because of their opinions in politics.

It was the same thing that had happened to Christina, especially for the fact that she worked in a male-dominated area. They criticized her several times without good reasons. Even through this, she was a determined winner.

George believed that eye for an eye is a way to go with an evil man. They deeply understood Christina's hard work in all this, her justice was not evaluated due to her skin colour.

Christina had started something, and it was for them to finish it, they couldn't afford to let her down. George survived through unofficial government deals. The moment he was released from prison after false accusations it meant dying to get his truth out and prove his innocence. He had no obstacles towards correcting his enemies.

Moreover, it was not the same feeling for Neil Hadebe, when he received a call at about three in the morning. They had left the hospital to another friend's place. One of their friends understood everything they were going through. When they asked for a helping hand, he provided it.

> We are not allowed to talk about it, especially if it is our own fathers. We call it a political error and parasite. We survived our father's iron hand by submitting to his rule. We are living in a world that is corrupt. Many things were stolen from our lands, but that did not stop misfortunes. We lost words and gave them to a dog to speak for us.

"Young rich people," nothing made them prouder than having it all before thirty years of age.

As they were sitting drinking whiskey on ice, Neil's phone rang. They all thought, "Who might this be calling in between such hours, unusual indeed." However, it was his mother, and she never called him at three in the morning before.

"Hello Ma," he said.

"Youngman, do you know sometimes we make decision endangering the people we love, and we end up in these bad positions. I will be waiting for you, and by the way your mother she is safe with me," a male voice said this on the phone.

This male voice belonged to an efficient hired gunman called Mr. Kong. He was working for the man Christina had arrested. A well-paid servant to complete the job, he was a living nightmare.

"WHO WAS ON THE PHONE? Mhazi asked. Neil exclaimed, "nobody, don't worry about it. Wrong number, I guess! "Seriously, who was on the phone? It cannot be a wrong number with everything turning upside down right now.

Who called you? Mhazi remained persistence about it, his strong instincts could tell that something was off.

"As I have said, nothing is wrong, just continue with sipping this syrup and whiskey." Neil had anger and pain expressions, at the same time his voice had changed, his tone was thundering when Mhazi asked about the caller. Neil poured some whiskey into his glass and Mhazi watched him.

"Give me the keys for your car? Neil asked Mark. They had two loaded guns in the car.

"We cannot help if you do not tell us what is going on! This is the time to open up and if you do not, whiskey will do no good for you, but to increase your problems," Mark took out his keys and placed them on the table.

However, our father's hearts are also broken, the only way to move forward is to let go and take the right decisions before a fetus of a pregnant woman is born. If we can give hope to a child in a womb, then we can give hope to infants also. We cannot build a future by teaching a womb child the art of war. It is not wrong to be different, because it is the uniqueness that changes the normality of daily beliefs. If Africa becomes one state, it will have advantages over poverty and control over resources.

"Someone is at my mother's place, and I think they are holding her captive." He opened up in tears.

"Did you recognize the voice of the person on the phone?

Mhazi asked to explore common suspects.

"No, I didn't recognize the voice, but I am totally sure, it is not friendly." Neil stood along with Mark.

Mhazi then said, "I am going with you, but because of the whiskey, I will rather drive."

Mark said to them, "I would love to help and go with you to your Moms, but Christina is still missing and I should look for her."

"We do understand your place and in any hope, if we both survive this, we expect to make business together in the near future," Neil said this. Mhazi took the keys and they left to Neil's hometown. They had two hours of driving non-stop, this was his chance to make things right.

The same officers that tried to kill Mark to do a cover-up for murder had kidnapped Christina. Someone approached them with a quality contract for Christina's head. They were paid almost half a million. They could not refuse the offer. These two took her out of the hospital with oxygen installed on a wheelchair.

It should be recognized that when the so-called "poverty" eradicates within a very short period of time, great consequences are near. Some are beyond the light and some above the light. We should start sacrificing the little we have to gain more. It is through sacrifice that hearts are put to test. Diamonds that were found in mines to protect and build legacies for people were taken by foreign companies leaving the indigenous of the land poor and inconsistent.

These officers moved her to an old building, reserved for dirty work. How can it be that money persuaded them into destroying one of their own?

Christina sat in this room unconscious for three hours. When they were not expecting her conscious, she gained it while they were in the middle of an argument about killing Christina.

Detective Anotida asked, "You know we have been paid to take care of her, are we doing all this to protect that old man from prison? These people are not doing all this just to cover up for someone. The former minister is doing this to hide something at large and my question remains, who are they trying to cover for? Or maybe the President." They laughed.

As they were aloud Christina heard them. After they had moved her from one place to another, she gained conscious when all hope was lost.

On the other hand, Foster and George were going through the files they had retrieved from the old man's house, these files had names of very large corporations doing businesses out of their boundaries. However, they were protected by higher-level government officials. The main reason for the deaths of many people were results of bribery. They seized a perfect opportunity to take out a corner of evil people and leaving many men in courts.

> Governments protecting minerals deployed soldiers into mines, and murdered innocent locals close to the mines, and making a living out of those minerals. It is a game played with few men betting on people's lives. It has one winning side with executives and shareholders of companies engaged with money laundry.

Christina observed these men while they were still in an argument. Although she had been unconscious for hours, they had chained her. One of the officers saw she had awakened, and he said, "Now, we have another problem, we cannot let her go anymore."

Detective Anotida replied, "relax, I bet she has no power at all. We can handle her, we have to shoot her, and then, we can go to collect half of the payment." Christina tried to take off her cuffs, but she had no strength at all.

"Don't even try, they don't come off easily," Detective Anotida said.

Christina started speaking to them, "you two should be ashamed of yourselves. I can't believe you two went this far. I do not matter anymore in this. Dead or alive, I will die with honor, unlike you two dirty scumbags."

"This would have been behind us if you had not intervened with our investigation. You cannot come here and start your own thing, remember we have families also. This is not something new to you or to anyone else. Even if we consider to let you go, still we are going to be hunted and slaughtered like animals, is that what you want Chris?

> Nothing is ever mentioned about workers brutally murdered in the name of protecting a business, in the case of Marikana in South Africa. Their families were left in pain, grievances and eager for answers. The drinking, drug use, dissatisfactions, broken marriages, adultery, lies, stealing, depression and isolation increases, money do not change these problems but only increases them.

These officers were totally caught in the middle of justice, although they were not small time thugs. They were perfectly caught under wrong commands. They cared less about justice and only focused more on riches. If the power is given to a man, it always seem as if it is bad at the end.

"Everyone is corrupt around here! You cannot tell me that by now someone hasn't offered you money. If we are going to let you go out of respect, you have to promise us that you will never come back."

Neil and Mhazi drove for about two hours, they arrived at Neil's old house at five in the morning. Neil stood in front of his mothers' house with dreadful fear to walk in. Nothing brought him more pain than to see his own mother in pain.

This was his center of weakness, and apologizing for all his mistakes was unlike him. She had cared for him and loved him.

IN THE CAR, THEY'D TALKED about busting caps and shooting everyone. They were ready to die, but that all sounded bogus. In front of his mother, he was not a street thug neither a rapper nor a busi-nessman, but a child. She was his softness, and some people knew that and used it against him.

''Let's go in, we cannot stand outside here all day, if this is the only way, then let it be,'' Mhazi remained a true friend.

Neil stood closer to the door, and he was not sure what to do, either to be his mother's son or a street soldier. Someone once told him the definition of a beef, a street grudge is bad when it involves your own mother. It is out of one's control when one's enemy reach-es to one's family.

> We are forever lost in the search for happiness. The solution for the poor is to understand Jesus Christ's courage to achieve a goal even through pain. We then understand the purpose of life, so we can constantly use faith. Many lives on earth, in general, are full of hard work, failures, and disappointments.

Neil was disadvantaged in the situation. His life had become the true definition of the war on home soil. They stole his strength away, only trepidation and tenseness could tell the end of the road.

He slowly opened the door. They walked into the house expect-ing her tied to a chair, but it was totally different, and it was not a hostage situation as he had assumed. They both came in one af-ter another. When they walked in, surprisingly, his mother and the man that had called him were watching television with coffee mugs in their hands. When Kong saw Neil, he said, "only one call from me, he comes running, didn't I told you so!"

Neil's mother was totally oblivious about everything. Afterward, they made greetings, his mother said, "He has told me everything about Jadea, and you should have told me earlier."

"Yeah sure, he did," with a very low voice tone Neil replied her, and added, "Can we please talk in private." These words were not referring to his mother. Although, she did sense the tenseness.

"We can speak here, we don't have to hide anything, do we? Whatever you want to say to me, you can also say it in front of your own mother," Mr. K replied.

Neil insisted on business, the man stood up and thanked Neil's mother for her coffee. They both went outside for a chat. Neil's mother strongly gazed at Mhazi, "Am I missing something here? She asked.

"My son is a troublemaker and I know him well, I gave birth to him, he is part of my curse and my blessing. Something is wrong out there, a business associate knocking at my door three in the morning looking for Nene, how important is that business with such bad timing? Tell me what is going on and do not lie to me." Instantly, Mhazi had a dry throat.

He answered her indirectly, "Whoever your son is today, he has a good heart. In prison, I was doing time for something I regret to this day. If I could take it all back, I would have done so. We were living in the same cell and for those few months, I had hope in my life after his wise counsel.

He taught me about life, and that people can actually change at some point. Through the valley of decision and the power of will, it was only after that when I started understanding there is more to life."

When she heard all these words, her nerves had calm. She started thinking otherwise, it was much more like the first time hearing something positive about her son. Neil grew up in the streets, in a ghetto that neighbors complained constantly about his miscellaneous behaviours. She went through a lot raising him. It is difficult for a woman to raise a man.

The two officers were determined to kill Christina, but it was too much to kill one of their own. She was not just any other cop; her work was highly rated by many people. As she was worried, these two officers left her in a bad condition that survival was ineluctable. They were both scared to put a bullet in her head. They abandoned her in a warehouse after she agreed to cut ties with them.

We lack a vast of knowledge, which is not found in the books we read, and yet we spend more time searching and revising the same notes.

Our knowledge is within us and it has access to power over nature. A system governed by people whose interests and ideas are only to feed a few families and it doesn't work properly for the governed. In a way, they keep on taking the public resources and tax to fund their own personal projects, which mostly have nothing to do with the benefit of the public that contributes taxation to the system. No government survives without people's help.

Chapter 18 - The Rich and the Poor

T HE TWO OFFICERS DROVE away from the warehouse. Their lives in the police work had been handling filthy work, it was only odd for them to do a good thing. Christina's tears were all over her face. She remained seated, powerless and weak, the little hope gave her strength and patience.

> It is said and done before the elections, but once the team wins, they abandon voters and peace-making, and mostly they make decisions that affect everyone dramatically. They do not show any interest in the constitution. They are topics that politician avoid in speeches during campaigns. It is true that lawmakers should abide by laws and never to live above them. When the time comes, remember in every generation revolutionaries and activists are born.

Neil took out the remaining diamonds out of his pocket. He gave Kong these diamonds, and he said, "If this is what you are for, then this is the last of it and you can have it all."

Mr. Kong replied to him, "this is not enough for your life, however, you are honest, and I have nothing against you. I have to admit that you are willing to go far to protect your own family. That is courageous."

Neil thought it was over, but this man further said, "Because I am letting you go, I have to warn you to stay away from cameras and police, don't get involved with them." Everything falls apart like a house built on sand after a strong wind.

WHILE MUGS WERE still in their hands, a gun was fired outside. People that were drinking coffee dropped their mugs out of shock. A bullet was fired into Neil's stomach. The gun sound made noise to the neighbors cleaning yards and some preparing to go to work. It was not a surprise to them that the sound came from Neil's house. They had expected it for a long time.

Although, Neighbours called the police under the assumption that it was a robbery. Mhazi and Neil's mother ran outside to help. They hurried to catch Neil lying on the door bleeding to death.

> They arise with a different understanding about history because in most cases, new generations are more educated than those before them. People are controlled because of food. Those that control food and water control people, but a person who controls the army controls guns. The hearts of leaders are also the hearts of men, they also fiend like other men do. Their desire for everything brings hardships on others.

"I cannot feel my legs," Neil repeatedly said. The man that shot him left in a hurry. Neil had believed in mercy, but these people showed no mercy and sympathy. When he gave away the diamonds as a peace treaty, it meant nothing to these people. They couldn't leave a target alive.

Mhazi reached first to Neil and covered Neil's wound with his jacket and pressure. He carried him to the car. They quickly drove to a local hospital. The pain that Neil felt wasn't from the wound, but his mother in tears.

She kept on telling him, "life is not a race, you are going to be okay." In the back seat of the car, she gently held him in her hands. She felt deep guilt of letting a killer into her home.

This woman wept for her child and constantly prayed. In her hands, Neil tried apologizing for lying to her.

He said to her, "This is not the way I had planned it."

She replied to him, "it is okay, do not worry at all."

They arrived at the hospital. The doctors and nurses helped them through. The wound was bad, as the bullet actually went on to affect his spinal cord, and from that point onwards, doctors engaged in an immediate operation. They tested HIV and AIDS before the surgery.

> Those that seek to control the world will never control it until they have captured all minds, assuming they do, revolutionaries are always born as well as peacemakers are also born. The only real change comes from within us, and it is not defined by a tribe that a person comes from or even a country or family. It is something found in us. When we value ourselves to change and do things differently, it means we can never reverse time and take control, but it is the only way to build something essential.

He had managed to keep the secret from his mother and Mhazi, but one of the doctors during the procedure spoke to his mother. He had two concerns. Firstly, Neil had lost a lot of blood and they needed more blood. Secondly, the spinal cord situation, they continued helping his body system to regain strength.

The woman didn't take the news about her son well. Mhazi opened his arms and held her closely. She wanted strength and someone to tell her something different. She murmured, "Why me, God?

THE DOCTORS WERE ABLE to take out the bullet. Neil's health insurance provided further assistance and security. Mhazi and the mother waited for more than three hours. Around past nine in the morning, the doctor came back alerting they'd stabilized everything, but Neil's chances of walking again were very little.

A nurse came along and urged them to go home and rest. They were both afraid to leave. Mhazi insisted on remaining behind.

"What if this bad man comes back? These were scary thoughts they could not handle. However, when they were still chatting together, Neil's sister arrived after receiving an immediate call. She arrived sweating and in tears.

> Police and army brutality left scares in many communities even after the colonisation revolution. Good men were caught up in wrong lines, and in most cases, they were ready to kill and destroy like soldiers deployed into the public to massacre citizens. We live in places where individuals are not aware of their own rights and voices, they are usually abused by officers without intentions of serving justice or whatsoever. They are after money and anything that can boost up their salaries or status. Those that vote for a certain government to be in place, they have a right to question its businesses for clarity.

What had happened made no visual sense, doctors allowed the whole family to see him after they'd finished with the blood transfusion process. The news about Christina's disappearance increased publicity at the police station, and nobody had answers to the actual story and facts. As usual, they all screamed, "we do not know."

Some demanded money in exchange with information. Marvin could not help further and his job was to keep his eyes on the prisoner. Nothing could replace that on his watch. The process to prosecute had begun, in terms of setting up the right judges and the right information, they were ready.

From the lowest to the highest, most provincial Judges were unjust. Christina hoped for justices after invading the retired minister's house.

A man living in a near-by shack found her and told other people that carried her to a hospital. A few days later, she was able to sit down and eat proper food. However, she often asked about a man who had helped. They looked everywhere for his details, but a man in a shack barely owns a birth certificate, it was just another long catch. George told the doctors to tell others to treat her secretly, assuming she was working for government agents.

> Soldiers brutalize people for power, instead of teaching them human rights in an undemocratic military state. People in this world suffer to get their hands on information necessary to change their lives. When a child has been raped, an officer accepts bribery, then what kind of a world are we living in? We are living in the days that the subject of high morals has been in question. We live in a world with Judges sending people away for a very long time, either innocent or guilty, the judgment is the same. More prisons are built to grow private companies.

She gave up trying to prove a point and focused on her healing. It was best for everyone to accept her sudden fake death and work hard to revenge her in their best interest. She had vengeance in mind. Her need to recover properly was essential. Like that, she was just better off for Detective Anotida.

Neil's life changed unexpectedly in a wheelchair. He was going to sit on that wheelchair for the rest of his life. Three weeks later, they released him from a hospital. The misery of his life was either to regret his fate or to move on and start afresh in the right direction.

George and Foster sponsored his music company. After the

hospital, he wanted a chance with the court, but everyone seemed against it. His girlfriend arrived from Mozambique and found him on a wheelchair. She felt helpless with only a few words of encouragement

WHEN THE COURT REVIEWED all the information pertaining to the former minister, he was facing more than twenty counts of fraud, murders and corruption, he was found guilty in all counts. George and Foster had enough information to bury this man. He was guilty of massacres, smuggling guns and all sorts of other charges followed.

The court did not procrastinate with the sentence for more evidence. This tied him to all his colleagues in power. His associates were more than twenty excluding police officers that were working for him. Soon after the main arrest, two homicide detectives disappeared from the picture and they were never found.

All his colleagues had powers of some sort, which included CEOs and other company executives.

He received a maximum of three life sentences after they'd raided his house again. It was just something that he could not escape anymore. They took over all the banks that had his name attached to it. It was a dark cloud in the country that took more than five weeks to settle down. A POWERFUL MAN HAD FALLEN.

Neil was able to start signing other young musician and write music for them, but as for him, he turned out well than expected. He rapped his music sitting on a wheelchair all the time, and his music transformed to gospel sound. They say people do not change, but in him, they found a new transformation.

Everything had changed and attentively, he focused on growing his business and telling his stories to other new musicians. So, they could understand that money is not everything. Some did listen and benefited from it.

He made a choice and decided to start taking the right path. He still had a son, unlike some of his role models. Some of them were in pursuit of a happy life by dancing with the devil and happiness was hard to find for them.

In conclusion, at the end of the day, we live in a ruthless world that has few good things than evil. It doesn't matter where we are, either in America, Africa, Europe, Asia or Australia, we will always find poor people in all these places. We live in a world that is led by immoral individuals, who always get what they want, whenever they want it. It might be religious, political or anything much close to it. People are controlled in masses due to fear and ignorance.

We cannot all be creative, we cannot all be strong and in that way, we have to understand those without strength. A superpower country usually operates as an oppressing hand.

It is like a marriage that can only work if both parties participate, if one is weak, the other should be very strong. We will always be one people and repression is part of human nature, it has been happening and it will always happen. Human beings are the same at heart, and good decisions separate us from our own demons. It is just a matter of time when a great country falls and another one rises with its philosophies and ideas.

We are likely to destroy ourselves over simple arguments about power. Billions are spent a year building integrated machines to destroy people. We are all focused on making a lot of money, that we cannot afford our own safety.

There is nothing as supremacy as long death prevails amongst us when we keep pushing each other into the corners. A corporation profit motive destroys a human consciousness to a point that families are increasingly divided over the high use of technology because of the dopamine business strategy.

THE AFRICAN LEADERSHIP system suffers from the fear to lose power, and it will always cause others to suffer over it. They talk about business, yet they do not own any. It is another question of thought, the difference between the old 'colonial system' and our new system is zero. People are not allowed to question the actions of leaders, yet they voted for those people. This is an offspring of the old system.

PEOPLE WILL SEEK greener pastures when life becomes hard on the other part of the town, knowledge should be written all over for people to read it and those that cannot read it, let them heal as others scream what is written on the wall. Life in this world has become hard for children and only God the Father, the Son and the Holy Spirit remains the hope.

MONEY IS NOT EVIL, but what people do for money and with money is evil. People continue to be enslaved by systems in places, labor slavery, and victims of mineral war. Political chaos is increasing as corruption dominates, the helpless are the poor. Religious and political affairs are powerful. Everything nowadays is business. The question to ask yourself is, what does it mean that Jesus Christ resurrected from death?

-For the Hip Hop generation, the dumbling down of black youth became commercialized, as mental mediocracy became a markerting scheme for the entertainment industry- the end.

Note: References;

For further reading:

1)http://themillenniumreport.com/2015/06/the-truth-about-gaddafislibya-na-tos-bombing-and-the-benghazi-consulate-attack/
2)https://chernobylguide.com/hiroshima_nagasaki/
3)https://www.amdigital.co.uk/about/news/item/red-rubber-atrocities-in-the-con-go-free-state-in-confidential-print-africa
4)https://crookedtimber.org/2011/03/23/interventions-humanitarian-or-liberal/
5)https://www.biblegateway.com/passage/?search=Proverbs%201&version=NKJV
6)https://www.biblegateway.com/quicksearch/?quicksearch=Matthew&version=NKJV
7)https://www.biblegateway.com/quicksearch/?quicksearch=romans&version=NIV
8)https://www.hrw.org/report/2009/06/26/diamonds-rough/human-rights-abus-es-marange-diamond-fields-zimbabwe
9)https://plato.stanford.edu/entries/confucius/
10)https://www.jstor.org/stable/2705391
11)https://www.pambazuka.org/pan-africanism/current-leaders-are-obstacle-unifi-cation-africa
12)https://www.mayoclinic.org/diseases-conditions/prescription-drug-abuse/symptoms-causes/syc-20376813#:~:text=Abusing%20prescription%20drugs%20can%20cause,or%20illegal%20or%20recreational%20drugs.
13)https://digitalcommons.du.edu/cgi/viewcontent.cgi?article=1553&context=etd
14)https://americanaddictioncenters.org/codeine-addiction
15)https://www.un.org/africarenewal/magazine/january-2006/african-migra-tion-tensions-solutions
16)https://thesentry.org/about/?gclid=Cj0KCQjwhb36BRCfARIsAKcXh6Gp9_VZL5T8cPTyYe5qfUWv5YBPmnFOHJFrjJ3JvnbTKZu-miUMPhAaAlqqEALw_wcB

ALL BIBLE VERSES in this book are quoted from NEW KING JAMES VERSION.

LEFT BLANK

www.ingramcontent.com/pod-product-compliance
Lightning Source LLC
Chambersburg PA
CBHW031952170626
46807CB00006B/2458